Betty Neels sadly passed away in 2001.
As one of our best-loved authors, Betty
will be greatly missed, both by her friends
at Mills & Boon and by her legions of
loyal readers around the world. Betty was a
prolific writer and has left a lasting legacy
through her heartwarming novels, and
she will always be remembered as a truly
delightful person who brought
great happiness to many.

This special collection of Betty's
best-loved books, are all available in
Large Print, making them an easier read
on your eyes, and ensuring you
won't miss any of the romance in
Betty's ever-popular novels.

The Betty Neels Large Print Collection

AN
ORDINARY GIRL
&
THE PROPOSAL

BY

BETTY NEELS

MILLS & BOON®

Pure reading pleasure™

BBC 22.8.08

AN ORDINARY GIRL
First Published in Great Britain in 1996
THE PROPOSAL
First Published in Great Britain in 1992
Large Print Edition 2008
Harlequin Mills & Boon Limited,
Eton House, 18-24 Paradise Road,
Richmond, Surrey TW9 1SR

AN ORDINARY GIRL © Betty Neels 1996
THE PROPOSAL © Betty Neels 1992

ISBN: 978 0 263 20468 1

Set in Times Roman 17 on 19¾ pt.
32-0808-53981

Printed and bound in Great Britain
by Antony Rowe Ltd, Chippenham, Wiltshire

CONTENTS

AN
ORDINARY GIRL

CHAPTER ONE

PHILOMENA SELBY, the eldest of the Reverend Ambrose Selby's five daughters, was hanging up sheets. It was a blustery March morning and since she was a small girl, nicely rounded but slight, she was having difficulty subduing their wild flapping. Finally she had them pegged in a tidy line, and she picked up the empty basket and went back into the house, where she stuffed another load into the washing machine and put the kettle on. A cup of coffee would be welcome. While she waited for it to boil she cut a slice of bread off the loaf on the table and ate it.

She was a girl with no looks to speak of, but her face was redeemed from plainness by her eyes, large and brown, fringed by long lashes beneath delicately arched brows. Her hair, tangled by the wind, was brown too, straight and fine, tied back with a bit of ribbon with no thought of fashion. She shook it back now and got mugs and milk and sugar, and spooned instant coffee as her mother came into the kitchen.

Mrs Selby was a middle-aged version of her daughter and the years had been kind to her. Her brown hair was streaked with silver-grey and worn in a bun—a style she had never altered since she had put her hair up as a seventeen-year-old girl. There were wrinkles and lines in her face, but the lines were laughter lines and the wrinkles didn't matter at all.

She accepted a mug of coffee and sat down at the table.

'Mrs Frost called in with a bag of onions to thank your father for giving her Ned a lift the other day. If you'd pop down to Mrs Salter's and get some braising steak from her deep-freeze we could have a casserole.'

Philomena swallowed the last of her bread. 'I'll go now; the butcher will have come so there'll be plenty to choose from.'

'And some sausages, dear.'

Philomena went out of the house by the back door, and down the side path which led directly onto the village street. When she reached the village green she joined the customers waiting to be served. She knew that she would have to wait for several minutes. Mrs Salter was the fount of all news in the village and passed it on readily while she weighed potatoes and cut cheese. Philomena whiled away the time peering into the deep-freeze cabinet, not so much interested in braising steak as she was in the enticing containers of ice cream and chocolate cakes.

Her turn came, and with the steak and sausages wrapped in a not very tidy parcel she started off back home.

The car which drew up beside her was silent—but then it would be; it was a Bentley—and she turned a rather startled face to the man who spoke to her across the girl sitting beside him.

'We're looking for Netherby House, but I believe that we are lost...'

Philomena looked into the car, leaning on the window he had opened.

'Well, yes, you are. Have you a map?'

His companion thrust one at her and she opened it out, pausing to smile at the girl as she leaned further in.

'Look, this is Nether Ditchling—here.' She pointed with a small hand, reddened by the cold wind. 'You need to go through the village as far as the crossroads—' her finger moved on '—go right and go to Wisbury; that's about three miles. There are crossroads at the end of the village. Go right, and after a mile you'll see a lane signposted to Netherby House. Can you remember that?' she asked anxiously.

She looked at him then; he had a handsome, rather rugged face, close-cropped dark hair and blue eyes. They stared at each other for a moment, and she had the strange feeling that something had happened…

'I shall remember,' he told her, and smiled.

Philomena gave her head a little shake. 'People often get lost; it's a bit rural.' She withdrew her head and picked up her steak and sausages from the girl's lap, where she had dumped them, the better to point the way on the map. She smiled as she did so and received a look of contempt which made her blush, suddenly aware that in this elegant girl's eyes she was a nonentity.

'So sorry. It's only sausages and steak.'

She didn't hear the small sound which escaped the man's lips and she stood back, hearing only his friendly thanks.

Her mother was still in the kitchen, peeling carrots. 'Philly, you were a long time...'

'A car stopped on its way to Netherby House; they'd got lost. A Bentley. There was a girl, very pretty and dressed like a fashion magazine, and a man driving. Mother, why is it that sometimes one meets someone one has never met before and it seems as though one has known them for always?'

Mrs Selby bent over the carrots. She said carefully, 'I think it is something which happens often, but people don't realise it. If they do then it is to be hoped that it may lead to happiness.'

She glanced at Philly, who was unwrapping the sausages. 'I wonder why they were going to Netherby House. Perhaps their eldest girl has got engaged—I did hear that it was likely.'

Philly said, 'Yes, perhaps that's it. They weren't married, but she had an outsize diamond ring…'

Her mother rightly surmised that the Bentley and its occupants were still occupying her daughter's thoughts. She said briskly, 'Will you make your father a cup of coffee? If he's finished writing his sermon he'll want it.'

So Philly went out of the kitchen, across the cold hall and along a passage to the back of the house, which was a mid-Victorian building considered suitable for a vicar of those days with a large family and several servants. The Reverend Selby had a large family, but no servants—except for Mrs Dash, who came twice a week to oblige—and the vicarage, imposing on the outside, was as inconvenient on the inside as it was possible to be.

Philly skipped along, avoiding the worn parts of the linoleum laid down years ago by some former incumbent, and found her parent sitting at his desk, his sermon written. He was tall and thin, with grey hair getting scarce on top, but now, in his fifties, he was still a handsome man, with good looks which had been passed on to his four younger girls. Philly was the only one like her mother—something which he frequently told her made him very happy. 'Your mother is a beautiful woman,' he would tell her, 'and you are just like she was at your age.'

They were words which comforted Philly when she examined her face in the mirror and wished for blue eyes and the golden hair which framed her sisters' pretty faces. But she was never downcast for long; she was content with her lot: helping her mother run the house, helping with the Sunday School, giving a hand at the various social functions in the village. She hoped that one day she would meet a man who would want to marry her, but her days were too busy for her to spend time daydreaming about that.

* * *

The driver of the Bentley, following Philomena's instructions, drove out of the village towards the crossroads, listening to his companion's indignant voice. 'Really—that girl. Dumping her shopping in my lap like that.' She shuddered. 'Sausages and heaven knows what else…'

'Steak.' He sounded amused.

'And if that's typical of a girl living in one of these godforsaken villages—frightful clothes and so plain—then the less we leave London the better. And did you see her hands? Red, and no nail polish. Housework hands.'

'Small, but pretty, none the less, and she had beautiful eyes.'

He glanced sideways at the perfect profile. 'You're very uncharitable, Sybil. Ah, here are the crossroads. Netherby is only a mile ahead of us.'

'I never wanted to come. I hate engagement parties…'

'I thought you enjoyed ours.'

'That was different—now we're only the guests.'

The house was at the end of a narrow lane. It was a large, rambling place, and the sweep before the front door was full of cars.

Sybil sat in the car, waiting for him to open the door. 'I shall be bored stiff,' she told him as they walked to the door, and he looked at her again. She was more than pretty, she was beautiful, with perfect features and golden hair cunningly cut. But just now she looked sulky, and her mouth was turned down at the corners. 'That stupid girl and now this…'

But once she was inside, being greeted by their host and hostess and the various friends and acquaintances there, the sulky look was replaced by smiles and the charm she switched on like a light. She was in raptures over the engagement ring, laughed and talked, and was the picture of a dear friend delighted to join in the gossip about the wedding. At the luncheon which followed she kept her end of the table entranced by her witty talk.

'You're a lucky fellow, James,' observed a quiet little lady sitting beside the rather silent man. 'Sybil is a lovely young woman, and so amusing too. When do you intend to marry?'

He smiled at her. 'Sybil is in no hurry, and in any case we're short-staffed at the hospital. I doubt if I could find the time. She wants a big wedding, which I understand takes time and organising.'

Kind, elderly eyes studied his face. There was something not quite right, but it was none of her business. 'Tell me, I hear that there is a scheme to open another ward…?'

'Yes, for premature babies. It's still being discussed, but we need more incubators.'

'You love your work, don't you?'

'Yes.'

She saw that she wasn't going to be told more and asked idly if he had enjoyed the drive down from town.

'Yes, it's a different world, isn't it? Last time I saw you, you were making a water garden. Is it finished?'

They turned to their neighbours presently, and then everyone left the table to stand around talking, or walked in the large formal garden, and it was there that Sybil found him presently.

'Darling, we simply must leave. I'm so bored. Say that you take a clinic this evening and that you have to be back by seven o'clock.' When he looked at her, she added, 'Oh, darling, don't look like that. It's such a stuffy party.'

She had a lovely smile, so he smiled back and went in search of their hostess.

Having got her own way, Sybil was at her most charming self, keeping up amusing talk as they drove back to London. As he slowed through Nether Ditchling she said with a laugh, 'Oh, this is the place where we talked to that plain girl with the sausages. What a dull life she must lead. Shall we be back in time to have dinner together somewhere I can dress up? I bought the loveliest outfit the other day—I'll wear it.'

'I must disappoint you, Sybil. I've a pile of paperwork, and I want to check a patient at the hospital.'

She pouted prettily, clever enough to know

that he wasn't to be persuaded. She put a hand on his knee. 'Never mind, darling. Let me know when you can spare an evening and we'll go somewhere special.'

He drove her to her parents' flat in Belgravia and went straight to the hospital—where he forgot her, the luncheon party and the long drive, becoming at once engrossed in the progress of his small patient. But he didn't forget the girl with the sausages. That they would meet again was something he felt in his very bones, and he was content to wait until that happened.

March had come in like a lamb and it was certainly going out like a lion. Winter had returned, with wind and rain and then the warning of heavy snow. Professor James Forsyth, on his morning round one Saturday morning, was called to the phone. 'An urgent message,' Sister had told him.

It was Sybil. 'James, darling, you're free this afternoon and tomorrow, aren't you? I simply must go to Netherby. I've bought a present for Coralie and Greg and it's too large to send.

Will you be an angel and drive me down this afternoon? I promise you we won't stay, and we can come straight back and dine somewhere. I thought tomorrow we might go to Richmond Park. The Denvers are always inviting us to lunch and I'm dying to see their new house.'

Professor Forsyth frowned. 'Sybil, I have asked you not to phone me at the hospital unless it is an urgent matter.'

'Darling, but this *is* urgent. I mean, how am I to get this wretched present down to Netherby unless you drive me there?' She added with a wistful charm which was hard to resist, 'Please, James.'

'Very well, I'll drive you down there and back. But I can't take you to dinner this evening and I need Sunday to work on a lecture I'm due to give.'

He heard her murmured protest and then, 'Of course, darling, I quite understand. And thank you for finding the time for poor little me. Will you fetch me? I'll have an early lunch. I can be ready at one o'clock.'

As they left London behind them the dark day became darker, with unbroken cloud and a rising wind. Their journey was half done when the first idle snowflakes began to fall, and by the time they were driving through Nether Ditchling it was snowing in earnest.

Sybil, who had been at her most charming now that she had got what she wanted, fell silent.

'Will ten minutes or so be enough for you to deliver your gift? I don't want to linger in this weather.'

She was quick to reassure him. 'Don't come in; I'll only be a few minutes. I'll explain that you have to get back to town.'

At the house she said, 'Don't get out, James. If you do they'll want us to stay for tea. I'll be very quick.'

She leaned across and kissed his cheek, got out of the car and ran up the steps to the front door, and a moment later disappeared through it.

The doctor sat back and closed his eyes. He was tired, and the prospect of a quiet day at home was very welcome. Peaceful hours in his study, making notes for his lecture, leisurely meals, time to read…

He glanced at his watch; Sybil had been gone for almost fifteen minutes. He could go and fetch her, but if he did they might find it difficult to leave quickly. He switched on the radio: Delius—something gentle and rather sad.

Sybil was sitting by the fire in her friend Coralie's sitting room. The wedding present was open beside them and there was a tea tray between them. Another few minutes wouldn't matter, Sybil had decided, and a cup of tea would be nice. While they drank it details of the wedding dress could be discussed…

She had been there for almost half an hour when she glanced at the clock.

'I must go. It's been such fun and I quite forgot the time. James will be wondering what's happened to me.' She gave a little trill of laughter. 'It's such a good thing he always does exactly what I want.'

She put on her coat and spent a few moments

examining her face in her little mirror. She added a little lipstick and went down to the hall with Coralie. Saying goodbye was a leisurely affair, too, but the butler had opened the door and she hurried out into the blinding snow.

The doctor had the door open for her. He leaned across to shut it as she got in and asked in a quiet voice, 'What kept you, Sybil? A few minutes was the agreed time.'

'Oh, darling don't be cross. I haven't been very long, have I? Coralie insisted that I had a cup of tea.' She turned a smiling face to him.

'You were half an hour.' His voice was expressionless.

Her smile disappeared. 'What if I was a bit longer than I said? I won't be ordered around and I won't be hurried. Now for heaven's sake let's get back to town.'

'That may not be possible.'

He drove carefully, for the snow was drifting and visibility was almost non-existent. The big car held the road well, but it was now pitch-dark and there was no lighting on the narrow country roads. He came to the crossroads, drove through Wisbury and onto the crossroads after it. It was as he drove into Nether Ditchling that a flashing blue light from a police car parked on the side of the road brought him to a halt.

A cold but cheerful face appeared at the window. The professor opened it and a policeman, muffled against the weather, poked his head in.

'Road's closed ahead, sir. Are you going far?'

'London.'

'Not a chance. They'll have the snowploughs out on the main roads, but they won't get here much before tomorrow afternoon.'

'Is there no other way? We've come from Netherby.'

'Just had a message that the crossroads at Wisbury are blocked. You'd best put up here for the night.'

Sybil said suddenly, 'I won't. I must be taken to London. Of course there's another road we can use…' Both men looked at her, and she added furiously, 'Well, do something, can't you?'

A tall figure in a hooded cape had joined them.

'Officer Greenslade? Can I be of help to you?'

'Reverend—I've suggested that these folk put up in the village, for they can't go anywhere else tonight.'

'Then let me offer them a meal and a bed.'

The Reverend Selby poked his head through the window in his turn. 'You car will be safe enough here. My wife will be delighted to help you.'

Professor Forsyth got out and made his way round to Sybil's door. 'That's most kind of you—we shan't be too much trouble?'

'No, no—and Greenslade, if anyone else needs shelter send them along to the vicarage.'

Sybil, for once mute, was helped up the short drive to the vicarage door and into the hall, where she stood watching the men shed their coats and cloak. She looked forlorn and very pretty, but the only feeling the professor had for her was one of exasperation. Nevertheless he unbuttoned her coat and took it off her, and then held her arm as they followed their host through the hall and into the kitchen.

This was a large room, with an old-fashioned dresser, a vast table with an assortment of wooden chairs around it and an elderly Aga giving out welcome warmth.

Mr Selby led the way to the two shabby Windsor chairs by the Aga, gently moved a cat and kittens from one of them, and said, 'My dear, we have guests. The road is closed and they can go no further.'

Mrs Selby gave them a warm smile and said, 'You poor things. Sit down and I'll make tea— you must need a hot drink.'

Professor Forsyth held out a hand. 'You're most kind and we're grateful. My name's Forsyth—James Forsyth. This lady is my fiancée, Miss Sybil West.'

Mrs Selby shook hands and turned to Sybil. 'This is horrid for you.'

Sybil lifted a lovely wistful face. 'Yes, I'm so cold and hungry, and we should be in London. If I could go to bed, perhaps I could have a small meal on a tray…'

James said evenly, 'You'll warm quickly here, and you have no need to go to bed.' He stopped speaking as the door opened and two girls came in, both fair-haired and pretty and smiling.

'We heard the car. Are you cut off from the outside world?' One girl offered a hand. 'I'm Flora and this is Rose. There are three more of us, but Lucy's spending the weekend with friends and Katie's finishing her homework. And Philly...'

A door at the back of the kitchen opened, letting in a great deal of cold air, and Philomena, wrapped in a variety of coats and scarves, with her head tied in some kind of a hood, came in.

'I got the chickens in, but we'll have a job to get to them by morning.'

She cast off some of the garments and looked across the kitchen at the tall man standing beside her father. 'Oh, hello, you were in that car...' She smiled at him and then saw Sybil, crouching by the Aga. 'And you, too,' she added cheerfully. 'Are you going to spend the night?'

She had taken off the last coat and pulled the hood off her head. 'I'll go and make up some beds, shall I, Mother? Rose will give me a hand.'

'Yes, dear.' Her mother was pouring tea into mugs and inviting the professor to sit down. 'Let me see. Miss…' She turned to Sybil with a smile. 'West, isn't it? You had better have Katie's room; she can go in with you. Rose and Flora can share, and Mr Forsyth…' Her eye fell on the bag he was carrying. 'Are you a doctor?' When he nodded, amused, she said, 'Doctor Forsyth can have the guest room.'

As Philly and Rose left the room she added, 'They'll put clean sheets on the beds, and if you're tired, which I expect you are, you can go to bed when we've had supper.'

'We are putting you to a great deal of trouble. Is there anything I can do?'

'No, no. It's stewed beef and dumplings, and there is plenty of it. Also there's an egg custard in the Aga.'

'Then if you've no need of Doctor Forsyth's services, my dear,' observed her husband, 'I'll take him along to my study while you and the girls get supper.'

There was the table to lay, more potatoes to peel, plates and cutlery to get from cupboards and drawers. Mrs Selby and Flora talked as they worked but Sybil stayed silent, fuming. A spoilt only child in a wealthy household, she had never done anything for herself. There had always been someone to wash and iron, cook meals, tidy her bedroom, to fetch and carry. Now she was dumped in this ghastly kitchen and James had left her with no more than a nod.

He would pay for it, she told herself silently. And if he and these people expected her to sit down and eat supper with them, they were mistaken. Once her room was ready she would say that she felt ill—a chill or a severe headache—and they would see her into bed and bring her something on a tray once she had had a hot bath.

Her thoughts were interrupted by a bang on the front door and voices. Philly ran to open it and returned a moment later with an elderly couple shedding snow and looking uncertain.

'Officer Greenslade sent them here,' announced Philly. 'They are on their way to Basingstoke.'

She began to unwind them from their snow-covered coats. 'Mother will be here in a moment. Our name's Selby—Father's the vicar.'

'Mr and Mrs Downe. We are most grateful...'

'Here's Mother.' Philly ushered them to the Aga and introduced them, and Flora pulled up chairs.

'A cup of tea to warm you?' said Mrs Selby. 'There'll be supper presently, and you'll sleep here, of course. It's no trouble. Here's my husband...'

The vicar and the professor came in together, and over mugs of tea the Downes reiterated their gratitude and, once warm, became cheerful.

Philly and her mother, busy at the Aga, rearranged the bedrooms.

'Rose and Flora can manage in Lucy's room; Mr and Mrs Downe can have their room.' So Rose went upstairs again, and then led Mrs Downe away to tidy herself and find a nightie.

It was time she dealt with her own comfort, decided Sybil, since James was doing nothing about it.

'I feel quite ill,' she told Mrs Selby. 'If I'm not being too much of a nuisance I do want to go to bed. If I could have a hot bath and just a little supper?'

Mrs Selby looked uncertain, and it was Philly who answered with a friendly firmness.

'No bath. There'll be just enough hot water for us all to wash—and if you go to bed now, I'm afraid we wouldn't be able to do anything about your supper for a bit.' She smiled, waving a spoon. 'All these people to feed.'

'But I'm ill…' Sybil's voice was lost in a commotion at the door again.

It was PC Greenslade again, this time with a solitary young man, his short jacket and trousers soaking and caked with snow.

'Got lost,' said the policeman. 'On his bike, would you believe it? Going to London.'

There was a general reshuffle as everyone moved to give the young man a place near the Aga. More tea was made and then the policeman, suitably refreshed, went back to his cold job while the young man's jacket was stripped off him.

He thanked them through chattering teeth. He was on his way to see his girlfriend in Hackney, he explained. He was a seasoned cyclist, rode miles, he added proudly, but like a fool he'd taken a shortcut recommended by a friend and lost his way…

'You poor boy,' said Mrs Selby. 'You shall have a hot meal and go straight to bed.'

Professor Forsyth said quietly, 'After a good rub down and dry clothes. You said that there will be no chance of a hot bath? He does need to get warm…'

The vicar spoke. 'If everyone here will agree, we will use the hot water for a bath for this lad. There will still be just enough for a wash for the rest of us.'

There was a murmur of agreement and he led the young man away.

'But *I* wanted a bath,' said Sybil furiously.

'But you're warm and dry and unlikely to get pneumonia,' said James, in what she considered to be an unfeeling voice.

The electricity went out then.

He told everyone to stay where they were,

flicked on the lighter he had produced from a pocket and asked Mrs Selby where she kept the candles.

'In the cupboard by the sink,' said Philly. 'I'll get them.'

There were oil lamps, too, in the boot room beyond the kitchen. He fetched them, lighted them, and carried one upstairs to the vicar and his charge. The people in the kitchen were surprised to hear bellows of laughter coming from the bathroom.

Philly had filled a hot water bottle, and when the Professor reappeared thrust it at him. 'He'll have to sleep in your bed,' she told him, and when he nodded she went on, 'I'll bring blankets down here and when everyone has gone to bed you can have the sofa. You won't mind?'

'Not in the least. Shall I take some food up? Clive—his name's Clive Parsons—is ready for bed.'

'Mother has warmed some soup. Katie can bring it up—she's the youngest. She's been doing her homework; she's very clever and nothing disturbs her until it's finished. But she should be here in a minute.'

'Homework in the dark?' he asked.

'She'll be reciting Latin verbs or something. I told you she was clever.'

The professor, beginning to enjoy himself enormously, laughed, received the hot water bottle and, presently back in the kitchen, devoted himself to improving Sybil's temper.

This was no easy task, for she had taken refuge in a cold silence, which was rather wasted as everyone else was busy relating their experiences in the snow and speculating as to what it would be like in the morning.

Presently the vicar came to join them. Katie had taken a bowl of soup with a dumpling in it up to Clive and had left him to enjoy it while they all gathered round the table.

The beef, stretched to its limits, was eked out by great mounds of mashed potatoes and more dumplings and was pronounced the best meal eaten for years. There was more tea then, and everyone helped to clear the table and wash up. Sybil's wistful excuses that she would like to help but she had to take care of her hands went unheeded. The professor, in his shirt-sleeves, washed the dishes while Mr Downe dried them and Mrs Downe and Mrs Selby found more candles and candlesticks.

Philly had her head in the kitchen cupboard and the girls were laying the table for breakfast.

'Porridge?' queried Philly to the room at large. 'For breakfast,' she added.

There was a general murmur of agreement but Sybil said, 'I thought porridge was what poor people in Scotland ate. I've never eaten it.'

The doctor said briskly, 'Well, now will be your chance. It's the best breakfast one can have on a cold winter's morning.'

She glared at him. 'If no one minds, I'll go to bed.'

Philly gave her a hot water bottle and a candle. 'I hope you feel better in the morning,' she said kindly. 'Remember about the hot water, won't you?'

The doctor abandoned the sink for a moment and went to the door with Sybil.

He gave her a comforting pat on the shoulder. 'You'll feel better in the morning,' he told her bracingly. 'We are very lucky to have found such generous kindness.'

He smiled down kindly into her cross face, aware that the feeling he had for her at that moment wasn't love but pity.

Sybil shook off his hand and turned to Katie, waiting to show her the way, and followed her without a word.

There had been a cheerful chorus of 'goodnight,' as she went, now followed by an awkward silence. The professor went back to the sink. 'Sybil has found everything rather upsetting,' he observed. 'She will be fine after a good night's sleep.'

'Which reminds me,' said Philly. 'Clive's in your bed. I'll get some blankets and a pillow for the big sofa in the sitting room. You're too big for it, but if you curl up you should manage.'

Everyone went thankfully to bed, leaving the professor, with one of the reverend's woolly sweaters over his shirt, to make himself as comfortable as possible on the sofa. As he was six foot four inches in his socks, and largely built, this wasn't easy, but he was tired; he rolled himself in the blankets and slept at once.

He opened his eyes the next morning to see Philly, wrapped in an unbecoming dressing gown, proffering tea in a mug.

Her good morning was brisk. 'You can use the bathroom at the end of the passage facing the stairs; Father's left a razor for you. The water isn't very hot yet, so I've put a jug of boiling water on the kitchen table for you.'

He took the mug, wished her good morning, and observed, 'You're up early.'

'Not just me. Rose has gone to wake the Downes, but we thought we'd better leave Clive until you've seen him—in case he's not well.'

'Very well. Give me ten minutes.'

In a minute or two he made his way through the quiet cold house. Someone had drawn the curtains back and the white world outside was revealed. At least it had stopped snowing...

He found the bathroom, shaved with the vicar's cut-throat razor, washed in tepid water, donned the sweater again and went to take a look at Clive.

He had recovered, except for the beginnings of a nasty head cold, and professed himself anxious to go to breakfast.

'No reason why you shouldn't. If you're still anxious to get to London as soon as the road's clear I'll give you a lift. We can tie your bike on the roof.'

With the prospect of the weather clearing, breakfast was a cheerful meal. The porridge was eaten with enthusiasm—although Sybil nibbled toast, declaring that she hadn't slept a wink and had no appetite. But her complaining voice was lost in the hubbub of conversation, heard only by the doctor sitting next to her.

'If the snowplough gets through we will be able to leave later today,' he told her, and then, hearing Philly saying in a worried voice that the hens would be snowed in, he volunteered to shovel a path to their shed.

So, in the vicar's wellies and with an old leather waistcoat over the sweater, he swung the shovel for a couple of hours. When he had cleared a path Philly came, completely extinguished in a cape, carrying food and water to collect the eggs. 'Enough for lunch,' she told him triumphantly.

The worst was over; the sun pushed its way through the clouds, the snowplough trundled through the village and they lunched off bacon and egg pie with a thick potato crust to conceal the fact that six eggs had been made to look like twelve.

The Downes were the first to go, driving away carefully, hopeful of reaching Basingstoke before dark. Half an hour later the doctor left, with a transformed Sybil, wrapped in her coat and skilfully made up, bestowing her gratitude on everyone.

The doctor shook hands all round and held Philly's hand for perhaps a moment longer than he should have, then ushered Sybil into the car, followed by Clive. They had roped the bike onto the roof and Clive, despite his cold, was full of gratitude to everyone. Well, not Sybil. He had taken her measure the moment he had set eyes on her, and why a decent gent like the doctor could be bothered with her he had no idea. He blew his nose loudly and watched her shudder.

The Bentley held the road nicely, but travelling at a safe speed they wouldn't reach London before dark. The doctor settled behind the wheel and wished that they had been forced to spend a second night at the vicarage, although he wasn't sure why.

CHAPTER TWO

SYBIL forgot her sulks as they neared London, and she ignored Clive's cheerful loud voice, too. She said softly, 'I'm sorry, darling. I did behave badly, didn't I? But, really, I did feel ill, and it was all so noisy. No one had any time for poor little me—not even you...'

She gave him a sidelong glance and saw with disquiet that he wasn't smiling. He was going to be tiresome; she had discovered that he could be. He assumed a remoteness at times which was a bit worrying. She was used to being admired and spoiled and she was uneasily aware that he did neither. Which was her reason for captivating him and—eventually— marrying him. She didn't love him, but then she didn't love anyone but herself. She was ambitious, and he had money and enjoyed a growing reputation in his profession, and above all she wanted his unquestioning devotion.

The doctor didn't take his eyes off the road. He said evenly, 'Yes, you did behave badly.'

Clive thrust a friendly face between them. 'Can't blame you, really,' he said. 'Not like the rest of us are you? I bet you've never done a day's work in your life. Comes hard, doesn't it?'

He trumpeted into his handkerchief and Sybil shrank back into her seat.

'Go away, go away!' she screeched. 'I'll catch your cold.'

'Sorry, I'm sure. Where I come from a cold's all in a day's work.'

'Do something, James.' She sounded desperate.

'My dear, I don't care to stop the car. What do you wish me to do?'

'Get him out of the car, of course. If I catch a cold I'll never forgive you.'

'That's a risk I shall have to take, Sybil, for I don't intend to stop until we get to your place.' He added gently, 'You will feel better once you have had a night's rest. Can you not look upon it as an adventure?'

She didn't reply, and very soon he was threading his way through London streets to stop finally before the terrace of grand houses where Sybil's parents lived.

He got out, warned Clive to stay where he was and went with her up the steps. He rang the bell and when a manservant opened the door bade her goodnight.

'Don't expect to be asked in,' said Sybil spitefully.

'Well, no,' said the Professor cheerfully. 'In any case I must get Clive to his friends.'

'I shall expect you to phone tonight,' said Sybil, and swept past him.

Back in the car, the Professor invited Clive to sit beside him. 'For I'm not quite sure where you want to go.'

'Drop me off at a bus stop,' said Clive, 'so's you can get off home.'

'No question of that. Which end of Hackney do you want? The Bethnal Green end or the Marshes?'

'Cor, you know your London. Bethnal Green end—Meadow Road. End house on the left.' He added gruffly, 'Me and my girl, we've got engaged, see? We're having a bit of a party…'

The doctor drove across the city's empty Sunday streets and stopped before the end house in a narrow road lined by small brick houses.

They got the bike down off the roof and Clive said, 'You will come in for a mo? Not quite your style, but a cuppa might be welcome?'

The doctor agreed that it would and spent fifteen minutes or so drinking a strong, dark brown drink which he supposed was tea while he made the acquaintance of Clive's girl and his family.

It was a pleasant end to a long day, he thought, driving himself home at last.

Home was a ground-floor flat behind the Embankment overlooking the Thames. The doctor parked the car, and before he could put his key in the house door it was opened by a short sturdy man with grizzled hair and a long, mournful face. Jolly—inaptly named, it had to be admitted—was the manservant whom the doctor had inherited with the flat, along with a charming stone cottage in Berkshire and a croft in the Western Highlands.

With the respectful familiarity of an old servant Jolly greeted the doctor with some severity. 'Got caught in all that snow, did you? Car's not damaged?'

'No, no, Jolly, and nor am I. I'm hungry.'

'I guessed you would be. It'll be on the table in fifteen minutes.' He took the doctor's coat and case from him. 'Found shelter, did you?'

'Indeed we did. At a place called Nether Ditchling—at the vicarage. Charming people. There were others caught in the snow as well—a houseful.' He clapped Jolly on the shoulder. 'I enjoyed every minute of it.'

'Not quite Miss West's cup of tea. She's not one for the country.'

'I'm afraid she disliked it, although we were treated with the greatest kindness.'

He picked up his letters and messages from the tray on the console table. 'Did you ring the cottage?'

'Yes. Plenty of snow, Mrs Willett says, but she's snug enough—hopes you'll be down to see her soon, says George misses you.'

The Professor was going down the hall to this study. 'I'll try and go next weekend. George could do with a good walk and so could I.'

Presently he ate the splendid meal Jolly had ready, then went back to his study to consider his week's work ahead. He had fully intended to phone Sybil, but by the time he remembered to do so it was too late. He would find time in the morning.

It was gone midnight before he went to his bed and he didn't sleep at once. He had enjoyed his weekend and he had enjoyed meeting Philomena. He smiled at the memory of her small figure bundled in that old hooded cape—and there had been a feeling when they had met—as though they had known each other for a long time…

Miles away, at Nether Ditchling, Philly turned over in bed, shook up the pillow and thought the same thing.

* * *

The snow disappeared as quickly as it had come. March came back with chilly blue skies and sunshine, and the banks beside the roads were covered with primroses. The vicarage became once again an orderly household.

There had been thank-you letters from the Downes, and a colourful postcard from Clive, and from Professor Forsyth a basket of fruit, beribboned and sheathed in Cellophane, with a card attached expressing his thanks. It expressed thanks, too, from Sybil—although she had told the doctor pettishly that she saw no reason to thank anyone for such a ghastly weekend.

'But you do what you like,' she had told him. Then, seeing his expressionless face, she had instantly become her charming self, coaxing him to forgive her. 'And take me out to dinner,' she had begged him. 'I've the loveliest dress, which I'm simply longing to wear…'

He had agreed that he would do that just as soon as he had an evening to spare. She was a woman any man would be proud to take out for the evening; he had no doubt that she would attract men's glances and he would be looked upon with envy.

The Professor, driving himself to the hospital later, told himself that he must make allowances for Sybil; she neither knew nor wished to know how the other half lived.

It was as though the weather had decided to apologise for that sudden return of winter. The fine weather continued, and even if the sunshine wasn't very warm it was bright. Philomena dug the garden, saw to the chickens, and ran various errands round the village for her mother. There was always someone who needed help or just a friendly visit.

Rose and Flora left home each morning, sharing a lift to and from the market town where Rose worked in a solicitor's office and Flora in an estate agent's firm. Dull jobs, both of them, but since Flora was engaged to the eldest son of a local farmer and Rose was making up her mind about one of the schoolmasters at the local prep school they neither of them complained since they had their futures nicely planned. Lucy was always busy with her friends, and as for Katie—the brightest of the bunch, the vicar always said—she had her sights set on university. It was a good thing, he often remarked to his wife, that Philly was so content to stay at home.

It was Monday morning again. The girls had left already and Philly had put the first load into the washing machine when someone thumped the front door knocker. Her mother was upstairs making beds, and her father was in his study, so she went to the door. It was someone she knew: young Mrs Twist from a small farm a mile outside the village. Philly had been there only a week before because Mrs Twist had needed someone to keep an eye on her twins while she took the baby to the doctor.

Philly swept Mrs Twist into the house. She had been crying and she clutched Philly's arm. 'Miss Philly, please help us. The doctor says the baby must go to London to see a special-ist—but there isn't an ambulance and he's been called away to Mrs Crisp's first. Rob can't leave the farm, so if you could watch the baby while I drive…'

'Give me five minutes. Go and sit by the Aga while I tell Mother and get a coat. What did the doctor say was wrong?'

'Possible meningitis. And there aren't any beds nearer than this hospital in London.'

Philomena raced upstairs and found shoes, coat and gloves, all the while telling her mother about the baby.

'You'll need some money. I'll tell your father…'

The vicar was in the kitchen comforting Mrs Twist and went away to get the money. 'You may not need it, but it is better to be safe than sorry,' he said kindly. 'I'll go to Mrs Frost and see if she knows of anyone who would go to the farm and give a hand. They had better not have anything much to do with the twins…'

Mrs Twist nodded, 'Yes, the doctor told me not to let them be with anyone.'

In the car she said, 'You're not afraid of catching it, Miss Philly? I shouldn't have asked you… Rob's got the baby at home, waiting for me.'

'Not in the least,' said Philly. 'Don't worry about a thing. Once baby's in hospital they'll give him all the right treatment.'

He certainly looked very ill and the small shrill cries he gave were pitiful. Philly sat in the back of the car with him while Mrs Twist drove the seemingly endless route to London.

Since neither of them knew the city well, finding the hospital took time, and although the rush hour was over there seemed endless stop lights and traffic queues. At the hospital at last, Mrs Twist thrust the car keys at Philly. 'Lock the car,' she said breathlessly. 'I'll take the baby.'

She disappeared into the emergency entrance and Philly got out, locked the car and followed her. Here at least there was speedy help; the doctor's letter was read, and the baby was borne away to a small couch and expertly undressed. Since Mrs Twist refused to leave him, it fell to Philly's lot to answer the clerk's questions. In no time at all there was a doctor there, reading his colleague's letter and then bending over the couch.

'Get Professor Forsyth here, will you, Sister? He hasn't left yet…'

Philly was making herself small against a wall. She supposed that she should find the waiting room, but she didn't like to leave Mrs Twist. She stood there feeling useless, hoping that she wouldn't be noticed: very unlikely, she reflected, since it was the baby who had everyone's attention. She admired the way Sister and the nurses knew exactly what they were doing, and she liked the look of the doctor, bending over the baby and talking quietly to Mrs Twist…

There was a faint stir amongst them as they parted ranks to allow a big man in the long white coat to examine the scrap on the couch.

Philly stared, blinked, and looked again. She had never expected to see him again but here he was, Doctor—no, Professor Forsyth, who had shovelled a path to her father's chickens wearing an old sweater of the vicar's and his wellies, looking quite different from this assured-looking man listening to the doctor.

He looked up and straight at her, but there was no sign of him recognising her. She had expected that; the baby had his full attention.

Please, God, let the baby get well again, begged Philly silently.

It seemed a long time before Professor Forsyth straightened his long back and began to give instructions. His patient was borne away in the arms of a nurse. He didn't go with them, but led Mrs Twist to a chair and leaned against the wall and began to talk to her. She was crying, and he looked across to Philly and said quietly, 'Will you come here, Miss Selby? I think Mrs Twist would be glad of your company while I explain things to her.'

He did this in a calm reassuring voice; the baby was very ill, but with immediate treatment there was every hope that he would make a good recovery. 'I shall stay with him for the next hour or so and he will be given every help there is. You will wish to stay here, near him, and that can be arranged. Do you need to go back home?'

'No, my husband can look after the twins. Can I leave my car here?'

'Yes. I'll get someone to see to that for you.'

Mrs Twist dried her eyes. 'You're so kind.' She turned to Philly. 'You don't mind? You can get a train, and someone could fetch you from the nearest station. And thank you, Miss Philly. Rob'll let you know if—if there's any news.'

'Good news,' said Philly bracingly. 'I'll go and see Rob as soon as I can.'

The Professor said nothing, but took Mrs Twist with him. Philly sat down to think. She would have to find her way to Waterloo Station, but first she must phone her father, for the nearest station to Nether Ditchling was seven miles away— and had she enough money for the fare?

She was counting it when a stout woman in a pink overall put a tray down on the chair next to her. 'Professor Forsyth said yer was ter 'ave this and not ter go until 'e'd seen yer.'

'He did? Well, how kind—and thank you for bringing it. It looks lovely and I'm hungry.' Philly smiled, prepared to be friendly.

'Yer welcome, I'm sure. Mind and do as he says.'

Philly ate the sandwiches and drank the tea, then went in search of the Ladies' and returned to her seat. There was no one else in the waiting room, although there were any number of people going past the open door and the noise of children crying and screaming. She wondered how Baby Twist was faring, and whether she would see Mrs Twist before she left the hospital. She looked at her watch and saw that she had been sitting there for more than an hour. But she had been asked to wait and it was still only mid-afternoon. There was no point in phoning her father until she knew at what time she needed to be fetched from the station. Besides, she was afraid to spend any money until she knew how much the fare would be...

It was another hour before the Professor came, and by then she was getting worried. She had been forgotten, the baby's condition was worse, and what time did the last train leave?

The Professor folded his length onto the chair beside her.

'Getting worried? I'm sorry you have had

this long wait, but I wanted to make sure that the baby would be all right...'

'He is? He'll get better? Oh, I am so glad. And Mrs Twist, is she all right, too?'

'Yes. How do you intend to get home?'

'Well, I'll go to Waterloo Station and get the next train to Warminster, and Father will come for me there.'

'Have you enough money for the fare?'

'Oh, yes,' said Philly airily. 'Father gave me ten pounds.'

He perceived that he was talking to someone who travelled seldom, and then probably not by train. He discarded his intention of a few hours of quiet at his home before going back to the hospital; he could be there and back in five hours at the outside.

He said, 'I'll drive you back to Nether Ditchling.'

'But it's miles away! Thank you all the same,' she added quickly.

'Not in the Bentley,' he observed gently. 'I can be back to take another look at Baby Twist later on this evening. He's in the safe hands of my registrar.' And when she opened her mouth to protest, he said, 'No, don't argue. Wait here for a little longer; I'll be back.'

She flew to the Ladies' once more, and was sitting, neat and composed, when he got back.

'Ready? Mrs Twist has asked me to speak to her husband; perhaps I might phone him from the Vicarage?'

'Of course you can.' She trotted beside him out of the hospital and got into the Bentley in the forecourt. She would have liked a cup of tea but she didn't dwell on that; he was wasting enough of his time as it was.

He had very little to say as he drove, only asked her if she was warm enough and comfortable. She made no attempt to talk; he was probably preoccupied with the baby's condition—probably regretting, too, his offer to drive her home.

It was a clear dry day, and once clear of the city he drove fast and she sat quietly, thinking her own not very happy thoughts: the poor little baby and his mother—and how would Rob manage with the twins? She would have to go and see him. And how she longed for a cup of tea and something to eat. That was followed by the even sadder thought that the Professor didn't much like her. Though I like him, she reflected, and it's a great shame that he's going to marry that awful Sybil. I wish I were as lovely to look at as she is…

The Professor turned off into the maze of narrow roads which would lead to Nether Ditchling. He was enjoying the drive, although he wasn't sure why. Philly, sitting like a mouse beside him and not uttering a word, was nevertheless the ideal companion, not distracting his thoughts with questions and trivial chatter. He slowed the car and turned into the Vicarage drive.

'You'll come in for five minutes and have a cup of coffee? We won't keep you, but you must have a few minutes' rest before you go back.'

He smiled at the matter-of-fact statement as he got out and opened her door. The Vicarage door was already open and her father stood there, telling them to come in.

'Come into the kitchen. Your mother's there, getting things ready for supper, Rose and Flora are upstairs, Lucy's at choir and Katie's seeing to the hens.'

He led the way and her mother looked up from her saucepans. 'Philly and Forsyth. Sit down. Coffee in a minute. Is the baby going to be all right—and why is Forsyth here?'

She put two mugs on the table and smiled at him.

'He's a professor,' said Philly.

'Is he now? But that doesn't make him any different,' said Mrs Selby, and he smiled at her.

'The baby will, I hope, recover. I work at the hospital where he is being treated. His mother is staying with him and it seemed a good idea, since I had an hour or two to spare, to bring Philly back home.'

Mrs Selby darted a look at Philly. 'We're very much in your debt…'

'No, no. Nothing will repay you for your kindness in the snow.' He drank some coffee and bit into a slice of cake. 'May I use your phone and talk to Mr Twist? He's been kept informed, but he might like a more detailed account of what's being done for his son.'

'In my study,' said the Vicar. 'Can we offer you a bed for the night?'

'No, thanks all the same. I want to get back and keep an eye on the baby.'

He took his coffee and the cake with him to the study and Mrs Selby said, 'What a very kind man…' She paused as Flora and Rose came into the room.

'We heard a car, and it's too soon for Lucy to be back from choir practice.' Rose sat down by Philly. 'Do tell, Philly. It's not the Twists' car, is it? The baby…?'

Philly, who had hardly spoken a word, explained, and Katie, who had just come into the kitchen with a pile of school books, exclaimed, 'Why ever did he bring you back home? He could have put you on a train. Is he sweet on you?'

Rose and Flora rounded on her, but Philly said calmly, 'No, Katie. He was kind, that's all, and I expect he feels he's now repaid Mother and Father for looking after him and Sybil when we had all that snow.'

The Professor, an unwilling listener as he left the study, had to smile at the idea of his being sweet on Philomena!

He left shortly afterwards, scarcely giving Philly time to thank him, brushing her gratitude aside with a friendly smile.

'You will get Baby Twist better, won't you?' she asked him.

'I shall do my utmost,' he assured her, as he took his leave.

The Vicar, after escorting him out to his car, came back indoors to observe warmly, 'Now there goes a man I should like to know better.'

Me, too, thought Philly.

She went the next morning to the Twists' farm and found Rob cautiously cheerful. He was a stolid young man, a splendid farmer and a hard worker, but he was unused to illness. He told Philly that he had had a phone call from his wife and that the baby was responding to treatment. 'I've got me mum coming today, to keep an eye on the twins and do the cooking.

And the doctor's been to have a look at them. He says they should be all right. They mustn't play with their friends, though, and they've got to stay here on the farm.'

'Well, I'll take them for a walk,' volunteered Philly. 'We can go picking primroses and violets. Has the Professor phoned you?'

'Late last night—must have been nigh on midnight—and then this morning at seven o'clock.'

He'd been up all night, thought Philly. He was a big powerfully built man, but all the same he needed his sleep like anyone else. She hoped that he would be able to snatch a few hours of leisure…

The Professor, despite a wakeful night, went about his usual hospital routine. He had gone home briefly, to shower and change, and returned looking as though he had had a good night's sleep to do his rounds, discuss treatments and talk to anxious parents.

Baby Twist, in a small room away from the other children, was holding his own; it wasn't for the first time that the Professor marvelled at the capacity of tiny babies to fight illness.

He left the hospital in the late afternoon and found Jolly hovering in the hall, his long face set in disapproving lines.

'Did you have your lunch?'

The Professor, leafing through his post, said casually, 'Yes, yes. A sandwich.'

Jolly pursed his lips. 'And your tea?'

'Tea? I had a cup with Sister after the clinic.'

'Dishwater,' said Jolly with disdain. 'There'll be tea in the sitting room in five minutes…'

The Professor said meekly, 'Yes, Jolly. How well you look after me.'

'Well, if I don't who will?'

The Professor didn't answer. He was very aware that Jolly disliked his future wife, although, old and trusted servant that he was, he would never allow his feelings to show, and his manner to Sybil was always correct. As for Sybil, she seldom noticed Jolly; he was part and parcel of James' life, a life which she had every intention of changing to suit herself once they were married.

A week went by. March gave way to an April of blue skies and warm sunshine and Baby Twist recovered; a few more days and he would be allowed home.

Mrs Twist had stayed at the hospital. How would she go back home? Sister wanted to know.

'Well, my car's still here, but I'm a bit scared to drive home without someone with me…'

Sister mentioned it to the Professor. 'She's a sensible young woman, but nervous of being alone with the baby—it's quite a long drive.'

'Perhaps she could contact the friend who came in with her?'

'Yes, of course. I'll see what she says. Had you a discharge date in mind, sir?'

'Four or five days' time—Wednesday. The baby will have to come back for a check-up. See to that, will you?'

It would be pleasant to see Philomena again. He hadn't forgotten her; indeed he thought about her rather more often than his peace of mind allowed. Her ordinary face and lovely brown eyes had a habit of imposing themselves upon his thoughts at the most awkward times: when he was dining with Sybil, listening to her light-hearted talk—gossip, tales of her friends, the new clothes she had bought— and dining with friends, listening to Sybil's high clear voice once more, her laughter... He avoided as many social occasions as he could, which was something she was always quick to quarrel about.

'And don't suppose that you can expect me to stay home night after night waiting for you to come home from the hospital or out of your study.' Then, seeing his frown she had added, 'Oh, darling James, how horrid I am. You know I don't mean a word of it.' And she had been all charm and smiles again.

On his way home from the hospital he made a note to himself to see Philly when she came to collect Mrs Twist and the baby.

Wednesday came, and with it Philly, very neat and tidy in a short jacket a little too big for her, since it was one of Lucy's, and last year's tweed skirt. But her shoulder bag was leather and her shoes were beautifully polished. The Professor saw all this as he watched her coming along the wide corridor to the ward. He saw her cheerful face too, damping down a strong feeling that he wanted to go and meet her and wrap his arms around her and tell her how beautiful she was.

'I must be mad,' said Professor Forsyth aloud, and when she reached the cot he greeted her with chilly politeness so that her wide smile trembled uncertainly and disappeared.

There was no reason to linger. Mrs Twist had her instructions and advice from Sister and an appointment to see the Professor in a few weeks' time.

The Professor shook Mrs Twist's hand and told her in a kind and reassuring voice that her baby had made a complete recovery. He stood patiently listening to her thanks before asking Sister to see them safely into the car and walking away. He gave Philly a cool nod as he went.

Sitting in the back with the baby as Mrs Twist drove back to Nether Ditchling, Philly wondered what she had done to make him look at her like that. She hadn't forgotten the strange feeling she had had when they had first met, but she didn't allow herself to think about it. She had been sure that he had felt the same, but perhaps she had been mistaken. And a good thing too, she told herself. She and Professor Forsyth lived in separate worlds.

In due course Baby Twist went back to London to be examined. Sloane, who had his surgery at Wisbury, was satisfied as to his progress, but the check-up was still advisable.

This time Mrs Twist took her mother, who was staying with them, on the journey to the hospital. Philly had hoped that she would be asked to go again. Even if she didn't speak to him, it would have been nice just to see the Professor again…

Professor Forsyth, giving last-minute instructions to Mrs Twist, firmly suppressed his disappointment at not seeing Philly. He really must forget the girl, he told himself, and dismissed her from his thoughts—although she persisted in staying at the back of his mind, to pop up whenever he had an unguarded moment.

He must see more of Sybil. He took time off which he could ill spare to take her out to dine and dance, to see the latest plays and visit friends and found that nothing helped. Sybil was becoming very demanding: expecting him to spend more and more of his leisure with her, scorning his protests that he had his own friends, lectures to write, reading to do...

Jolly, disturbed by the Professor's withdrawn manner, gave it as his opinion that he should go to his cottage. 'You've got a bit of free time,' he pointed out. 'Go and see Mrs Willett. She's always complaining that she doesn't see enough of you. And that George will be pining for you too.'

The Professor went home on Friday evening with the pleasant knowledge that he had two days of peace and quiet to look forward to. Sybil had said that she would be away for the weekend and he planned to leave early on Saturday morning. He ate a splendid dinner and went to his study; there was plenty of work for him on his desk.

He hadn't been there more than ten minutes when the phone rang.

It was Sybil's querulous voice. 'The Quinns phoned. That wretched child of theirs has got chicken pox—they told me not to worry, as she's in the nursery anyway, but I'm not risking catching it. So I'm here at a loose end, darling. Take me out to dinner tomorrow evening and let's spend the day together first. Come for me around midday. We can go to that place at Bray for lunch and drive around. And on Sunday you could drive me up to Bedford. We can spend the day with Aunt Bess. It will be a dull day, but she's leaving me the house when she dies and we shall need somewhere in the country as well as your place here.'

'I have a cottage in Berkshire, Sybil…'

She gave a little crow of laughter. 'Darling! That poky little place! There would barely be room for the two of us, let alone guests.'

The Professor pondered a reply but decided

not to say anything. Instead he said, 'I'm sorry about your weekend, Sybil. I'm going out of town early tomorrow morning and I shan't be back until Monday. A long-standing invitation.' Which was true. Mrs Willett, his one-time nanny and housekeeper at the cottage, reminded him almost weekly that it was time he spent a few days at the cottage.

'Put them off,' said Sybil.

'Impossible. As I said, it's a long-standing arrangement.'

She hung up on him.

He left early the next morning, taking the M4 until he had passed Reading, then turning into a side road running north to the Oxfordshire border. The villages were small and infrequent, remote from the railway, each one with its church, main street and a handful of small houses and cottages. And each with its manor-house standing importantly apart.

The country was looking beautiful in the bright morning sun and the Professor slowed his pace the better to enjoy it. He didn't come often enough, he reflected. But Sybil didn't like the cottage and the quiet countryside, and she didn't like Mrs Willett who, for that matter, didn't like her either.

The cottage was on the edge of a village lying between two low tree-clad hills, round the bend of the road so that the sudden sight of it was a pleasure to the eye. Beyond a narrow winding street bordered by other cottages stood his own: redbrick and thatch, with an outsize door and small-paned windows. It stood sideways onto the road, with a fair-sized garden, and beyond it were fields and, beyond them, the wooded hill.

He drove round the side of the cottage to a barn at the end of the track, its doors open ready to receive him, and parked the car and went into the cottage through the open kitchen door.

The kitchen was small, with a tiled floor, a small bright red Aga and shelves along its walls. There was a table in the centre, with a set of ladder-backed chairs round it. There were bright checked curtains at the window and a kettle was singing on the stove.

The Professor went through the door into the narrow hall, threw his jacket and bag down on one of the two chairs and hugged his housekeeper, puffing a little from her hasty descent of the narrow stairs.

'There you are, Master James, and about time too!' She eyed him narrowly. 'You look as though you could do with a few days here. Working too hard, I'll be bound.'

'It's good to be here,' he told her. 'I'll stay until early Monday morning. Where's George?'

'Gone to fetch the eggs from Greggs' farm with Benny.' Benny was the boy who walked George each day, since Mrs Willett was past the age of a brisk walk with a lively dog.

'I'll go and meet them while you get the coffee.' He grinned at her. 'We'll have a good gossip.'

'Go on with you, Master James! But I dare say you'll have plenty to tell me.' She gave him a questioning look. 'Fixed a date for the wedding yet?'

His soft, 'Not yet, Nanny,' left her with a feeling of disquiet.

Later, with George the Labrador pressed up against him, the Professor gave Mrs Willett a succinct enough account of his days. 'Rather dull, as you can see,' he told her. 'Except for that weekend at the Vicarage.'

She had watched his face when he told her about it, and had been quick to see the small smile when he'd told her about Philly.

'A real country girl,' she had observed mildly.

'You would like her, Nanny.'

'Then it is to be hoped that I'll meet her one day,' said Nanny.

CHAPTER THREE

AT DAYBREAK on Monday morning the Professor, with George at his heels, let himself out of the cottage, opened the little gate at the bottom of his back garden and started to climb the gentle hill beyond. Halfway up it he stopped and turned to look behind him. It was a bright morning and the sun was going to show at any moment. The cottage sat snugly in its garden and the white curtains at his bedroom window waved gently to and fro in the light breeze. A little haven, he reflected, and one to which he should come far more frequently. But Sybil had been adamant about not going there, always coaxing him to stay in town when he had a free weekend—'For I see so little of you,' she had said, beguiling him with one of her charming smiles.

The Professor turned to continue his walk. There was a tractor starting up some way off, a herd of cows leaving the milking shed from the farm across the fields, everywhere birds, rabbits in the hedges and, sneaking across the field ahead of him, a fox. He wanted to share it all with someone—with Philly, for this was her kind of world.

'I don't even know the girl!' said the Professor testily, and resumed his walk.

He drove himself back to London after breakfast, thinking of the busy day ahead of him, and the days after that, and at the weekend he and Sybil were going to Coralie's wedding at Netherby. Perhaps on the way back he could persuade her to go to the cottage for an hour or two...

But Sybil was adamant about that, too; she had bought a new outfit for the wedding and she had no intention of ruining it by paying a visit to the cottage with a chance of tearing it on hedges or having George's dirty paws all over it. 'And it was wickedly expensive, darling. I want to be a credit to you, and I've gone to a great deal of trouble.'

So on Saturday morning the Professor, elegant in morning dress and top hat, bade Jolly goodbye and drove to collect Sybil—who wasn't ready.

The butler, a sympathetic man, ushered him into a small room and offered coffee, assuring him that Miss Sybil would be down directly. And half an hour later she did indeed come downstairs. She stood in the doorway, waiting for the Professor's admiration. Her dress was white, with a vivid green pattern calculated to catch the eye, but it was her hat which kept him momentarily silent.

Of bright green straw, it had an enormous brim and the crown was smothered in flowers of every colour.

'Well?' said Sybil. 'I told you the outfit was gorgeous, didn't I? It's charming, isn't it?'

The Professor found his voice. 'All eyes will be upon you.'

She smiled happily. 'That is my intention, James darling.'

'I thought the bride was the principal attraction on her wedding day.'

'There's nothing like a little healthy competition, darling.'

They drove for the most part in silence: the Professor deep in thought, Sybil contemplating the pleasures ahead of them. They must get seats in the church where she would be easily seen, and stand well to the front when the photos were taken…

Approaching Nether Ditchling, the Professor slowed the car; there was the chance that he might see Philly. And the chance was his; there she was, standing outside the village shop. No hat on her head, but wearing what he suspected was her best dress: blue, simply cut, and off the peg.

He pulled the car across the road and stopped beside her. He rolled the window down. 'Hello, Philomena. Are you going to the wedding too?'

Philly beamed at him; thinking about him was one thing, to see him was an added bonus. 'Hello.' She looked past him to Sybil, and her eyes widened at the sight of the hat. She met the Professor's gaze and it was as though they shared the same thought. Philly looked away from him and wished Sybil good morning.

'Oh hello, nice to see you again. We're in rather a hurry…'

'Are you going to the wedding?' asked the Professor again.

'Well, yes, but not really to the wedding. I promised Coralie that I'd look after her sister's small children. There are four of them, much too small to go to the church and the reception.'

'In that case we'll give you a lift.' The Professor got out of the car and opened the door.

Philly held back. 'I was going to get a lift from the postman; he'll be along any minute now…'

'Leave him a message,' said the Professor easily, and did it for her, charming Mrs Salter standing at the open shop door, listening to every word.

She nodded and smiled. 'You go, Miss Philly. Not often you get the chance to travel so grand. I'll tell Postie.'

The Professor made small talk during the

brief journey to Netherby and Philly said, 'Yes' and 'No' and 'how nice,' and admired the back of his head, and then turned her attention to Sybil's hat. Wedding hats, she knew, were always outrageous, but Sybil's took one's breath…

'Go straight to the church,' said Sybil. 'We want decent seats…'

The Professor said mildly, 'We are in plenty of time, my dear. I'll drop Philly off at the house on the way to church.'

'There's no need. It's only a short walk…'

He disregarded that. 'How will you get back?' he asked Philly.

'Father will fetch me.'

At the house there were a number of cars being loaded by the family on their way to the church, so Philly nipped out smartly. 'Thank you very much—I hope you'll have a lovely day.'

She whisked herself away and in through the open doors, and Sybil said, 'Oh, for heaven's sake, let's get to the church.'

* * *

Seedings, the butler, bade Philly a dignified good morning. 'Miss Coralie would like you to go to her room, Miss Philly, as soon as you get here.'

So Philly went up the grand staircase and tapped on a door. She was admitted, to spend five minutes admiring the bride and the bridesmaids, before going up another flight of stairs to the nursery wing with Coralie's sister.

'Just like Nanny to become ill when she's most needed. I'm very grateful, Philly.' She opened a door. 'Mother's maid is with them…'

There were twins, not quite four years old, Henry and Thomas, Emily, almost two and the baby, a mere eight months. At the moment they looked like small angels, but it was still early in the day. Philly, though she liked small children, braced herself for the task ahead.

The wedding was at eleven o'clock. She heard the church bells pealing at the end of the service and presently the slamming of car doors as everyone returned to the house. There would be any number of guests, she knew. Friends and family would come from far and near to enjoy the occasion. She hoped that Coralie would be very happy; they could hardly be described as friends, they didn't move in the same circles, but Philly had been at school with Coralie's sister, the eldest of the three girls, so they were on friendly terms.

A maid brought the children's lunch, and soon the baby was due for another bottle. Philly assembled her small companions round the nursery table and for the moment forgot about the wedding.

No one came, but she hadn't expected anyone. She had told the maid to tell the children's mother that everything was going well, and now she settled the eldest three little ones to an afternoon nap. She set about seeing to the baby, who refused to be settled but lay on her shoulder, bawling his small head off.

The opening of the door brought his crying to an abrupt halt. He burped, puked on her shoulder, and smiled at the Professor entering the room.

'I'll have him while you clean up.'

'You can't possibly—look at you in your best clothes. You ought not to be here.'

He grinned at her, wondering why it was that when he was with Philly he felt life was such fun. 'I'm on an official visit,' he told her. 'I had the twins in for a few days with bad chests, and I've come to see if they're fit and well again.'

'They're asleep.' She nodded to where they lay, tucked up in one of the cots. 'They've been as good as gold and they ate their lunch.'

The baby was taken from her. 'Good. Go and wash while this monster's quiet.' He took the baby from her in the manner of a man who knew exactly what he was doing. But then he would, she reflected, scrubbing at her dress; he was a children's doctor.

'Was it a lovely wedding?' she asked.

'Yes. The bride looked beautiful, as all brides do.'

'Shouldn't you be at the reception?'

'The cake's been cut and toasts have been drunk, and everyone is standing around waiting for the happy couple to leave. How are you going home?' he asked again.

He was sitting on the arm of a chair, the baby peacefully asleep against his waistcoat.

'Father will come for me.'

'Better still, we'll drop you off as we go.' He had a phone in his hand and was dialling a number. Philly, aware that she should remonstrate with him at such high-handed behaviour, said nothing, listening to him telling her father that she would be returning in about an hour or so.

'I can't go until someone comes to look after the children,' said Philly, finding her voice.

'There'll be someone,' he assured her, and smiled, handed back the baby and went away.

'Well, really. I don't know,' said Philly to the baby, who stared back at her and went to sleep again.

Philly longed for a cup of tea, but she had no doubt that she had been forgotten with the house full of guests and everyone run off their feet. She drank some water and looked at the nursery clock; in less than an hour the children's tea would be brought up, and then hopefully someone would come to take her place.

She worried a bit about the Professor giving her a lift. For one thing Sybil wouldn't like it, and for another she might keep them waiting unless someone took over promptly.

The children woke up, and she washed their faces and hands, brushed their hair and sat down on the floor with them to play the nursery games she remembered from her childhood, thankful that the baby remained soundly asleep. Their teatime came and went, and after another ten minutes she picked up the phone. Just as she did the door opened and a maid came in with a tray.

'Sorry I'm a bit late, Miss. Everything's a bit rushed downstairs. The guests are leaving. Here's a pot of tea for you.'

Philly beamed at her. 'Thank you. I'm sure you are rushed off your feet. I expect someone's coming to take over?'

'I don't rightly know, Miss.'

Which wasn't very satisfactory. Philly sat the children at the table, put the baby's bottle ready to warm and handed out mugs of milk and egg sandwiches, much cheered by the sight of the teapot, but before she could pour herself a cup the door opened and the children's mother came in.

'What a day! I'm exhausted, but it all went off splendidly. Are you ready to go?'

An elderly woman came in behind her. 'We'll see to the children now. Have they been good? We are so grateful, Philly. Now do run along; James and Sybil are waiting for you.'

They bustled her away. She bade the children a hurried goodbye, with a regretful look at the teapot, smiled away their mother's thanks, and hurried down to the hall. The Professor was there, talking to a group of guests, but when he saw Philly he made his goodbyes and crossed the hall to meet her.

'I've kept you waiting?'

He smiled down at her. She looked tired and dishevelled, and her hair badly needed a comb; he found it disturbing that she outshone all the attractive women he had seen that day. And that included Sybil.

'The car is outside,' he told her. 'You must be tired.'

'Well, a bit.' She smiled in the general direction of everyone else there and walked to the door, feeling very out of place. At the door she was stopped by the butler, who handed her a neatly wrapped package.

'Wedding cake, Miss—I was to be sure and give you a slice. For good luck, you know.'

She thanked him and got into the car, where Sybil said, 'There you are at last. James, I'm exhausted…'

'Not nearly as exhausted as Philly after most of the day spent with a handful of toddlers and a baby.' He looked over his shoulder. 'All right? We'll have you home in no time.'

Philly had settled on the back seat, bringing with her a strong whiff of baby talcum powder, milky drinks and soap. There were sponged stains on her dress, which from time to time gave off an unavoidable tang. Sybil gave an audible sigh and the Professor bit back a laugh.

No one spoke on the brief journey. At the Vicarage he got out and opened her door. Not sure if she would receive a snub, Philly offered tea.

'I know Mother will be delighted…'

'In that case we would be delighted; a cup of tea is just what I need. Don't you agree, Sybil?'

She shot him a look which boded ill for the future, but she got out of the car and Philly ushered them into the Vicarage.

She took them not to the kitchen but into the drawing room, which was seldom used because it was always damp, even in the height of summer. It was a splendid room, with wide windows, and furnished with the good pieces her mother had inherited when her parents died. A fitting background for Sybil's hat, thought Philly naughtily.

'I'll tell Mother,' said Philly, and sped to the kitchen.

Mrs Selby, being a vicar's wife, was unflustered by sudden demands on her hospitality.

'Fetch your father,' she said, and went to welcome her visitors.

Leaving the Vicar to entertain them, Mrs Selby hurried back to the kitchen, where Philly was putting cups and saucers onto a tray.

'That's the most extraordinary hat,' she observed, getting a cake from its tin, and added, 'She's not at all suitable…'

Philly giggled, and then said, suddenly sober, 'But she does look gorgeous, Mother.' Adding matter-of-factly, 'She doesn't like me.'

'No, dear. But of course that is only natural.'

Philly made the tea. 'Is it? Why?'

Her mother didn't answer. 'Bring the teapot, dear. I'll take the tray.'

The Professor had quite a lot to say about the wedding, but Sybil hardly spoke and refused Mrs Selby's fruit cake with an, 'Oh, God no,' which made the Vicar draw a breath and bite back the rebuke on his tongue.

Mrs Selby filled an awkward moment by observing cheerfully, 'I expect you had too much wedding cake. A wedding wouldn't be one without it, though, would it?' She turned an artless gaze onto Sybil. 'Have you planned your own wedding? I dare say it will be a big one?'

'Oh, I suppose so. We have very many friends. Though we don't intend to marry yet…' Sybil's vague reply, from Mrs Selby's point of view, was reassuring…

They didn't stay long, but their departure was delayed for a few minutes by the arrival of Lucy and Katie, back from their schools. They wanted to hear about the wedding, and Katie remarked with all the candour of a teenager upon Sybil's hat. It was fortunate that Sybil, confident of her splendid appearance, took Katie's, 'Now that's what I call a hat…' as a compliment.

Sybil said, in the voice she used to those beneath her notice, 'I'm glad you like it. I had it specially made…'

The Professor, looking amused, shook hands all round and ushered her into the car.

Driving away, Sybil said, 'I can't think why you had to stop. There was no need to give that girl a lift—she smelled…'

'Philly has spent most of the day looking after three toddlers and a small baby. They needed to be fed and washed and cuddled and amused. A hands-on job, Sybil, without regard to what one is wearing.'

'You should have considered me. I hate anything like that…'

'Would you even with your own children?'

'We will have a highly qualified nanny—and anyway, I consider four children to be excessive. One is more than enough. Shall we be back in time to go out to dinner? A pity you can't join me at the Reeves' for lunch tomorrow. Really, you take your work too seriously, James.'

The Professor reflected that falling in love with a lovely face had been a mistake. One which he would have to rectify if he could think of a way of doing so.

Sybil didn't love him; he had thought at first that she did, but now he realised that loving someone was very low in her priorities. There were things which mattered more: comfortable living, money, being popular amongst the society in which she moved, a husband with money to spend on her—and one who was at the top of his profession—and the leisure to enjoy her life without worry.

He said now, 'It will be eight o'clock

before we're home, and I want to go to the hospital. And I'm sorry about tomorrow but there's this meeting…'

'How tiresome you are, James. But we'll change all that when we're married.'

'Am I to give up my work?'

'Don't be silly, of course not. But you can give up all this hospital work and keep your private practice. Do some consulting work, if you must, but you're well enough known to pick and choose.'

'I'm a children's doctor, Sybil, and that's what I intend to remain.'

Sybil gave a little laugh. 'Darling, I'll change your mind for you.'

The Professor didn't answer.

After leaving Sybil at her home, he drove straight to the hospital. There was a premature baby he wasn't happy about, and he spent the next hour or so discussing treatment with his registrar.

It was ten o'clock before he got home and Jolly, coming into the hall as he let himself in, said, 'There you are then, and high time too.

It's a good thing your dinner's one that won't spoil.' He peered at the Professor. 'Fed up with the day? Weddings, leastways anyone else's but yours, aren't much cop.'

The Professor had one foot on the stairs. 'Give me five minutes to get into other gear. I could eat a horse, Jolly.'

'Not in this house, you won't. I don't hold with horseflesh!'

The professor laughed. Five minutes later he was back again, in casual trousers and a sweater, pouring himself a whisky.

No one looking at Jolly would have thought of him as being an excellent cook. But he dished up a splendid meal, and the Professor, whose large frame needed more than the bits and pieces usually offered at weddings, enjoyed every morsel of it.

'That's the ticket,' observed Jolly. 'Be in for lunch tomorrow, will you?'

'As far as I know. I think I'll drive down to the cottage in the afternoon. If you want to go out, leave something cold for me, Jolly. I'll probably stay there for tea.'

'Miss West going with you?'

The Professor said, 'No,' in a voice which warned Jolly not to say any more.

Sunday was a dry day, but cold under a grey sky. The cottage looked charming, with daffodils spilling from the banks around it and great clumps of primroses. There were early tulips in the flowerbed and forsythia in abundance. George was delighted to see him and Nanny, roused from an afternoon nap, bustled about getting tea. The Professor, greeting them both, wished that Philly was there, too. It was becoming increasingly evident to him that she fitted very nicely into the kind of life that he enjoyed...

Easter had been early and May Day wasn't far away. Nether Ditchling was preparing for the annual children's fête which would be held on Bank Holiday Monday. It was held in the village hall, lavishly decorated with balloons, and was an old-fashioned event, its traditions untouched by modern ideas.

There would be Punch and Judy, in the disguised persons of the primary schoolmaster and his wife, a bran-tub, presided over by Mrs Salter, a trestle table loaded with buns and ices, lemonade and bags of crisps donated by Lady Dearing, wife of the Lord of the Manor, and served by herself and her two daughters, while at the other end of the hall her son would be in charge of target shooting with toy rifles.

Since the children would have their mothers and fathers with them, the Vicar and his wife always took charge of a vast tea urn, rows of cups and saucers and a great variety of cakes. As for Philly and her sisters, they helped out wherever they were needed: consoling crying children, taking toddlers to the lavatory, clearing up after one of them had eaten too much. It was an event which never varied from year to year and no one would have wanted it otherwise. This year there was to be a fancy dress parade with prizes, which meant a good deal of searching in trunks and attics and a run on the crinkle paper which Mrs Salter had remaining in stock from Christmas.

The church was full on the Sunday before.

The Lord of the Manor with his wife and family sat in their high-walled pew, and the Vicar's wife and his five daughters were on the other side of the aisle. Rose and Flora had their fiancés beside them, and Lucy's current boyfriend sat there too. Only Katie and Philomena were unaccompanied, and as usual the village craned its neck to see if Miss Philly had found a man yet. The nicest of the bunch, everyone agreed, but likely to die an old maid.

Philly, unaware of the village's concern for her future, sat quietly, listening to her father's sermon, while hidden away at the back of her mind she wondered what the Professor was doing.

He, just as she was, was in church. Sybil had gone to Italy for a week to stay with friends who had a villa in Tuscany. It was an invitation she couldn't ignore, she had told him. She had sounded regretful, peeping at him to see if he minded, but his face had told her nothing and she had been careful to beg him to go with her. 'I see so little of you, darling, and we could have a lovely time. There'll be several people we both know there, and there'll be plenty of amusement.'

When he had said patiently that a holiday for him was out of the question she had made a charming little face and said, 'Surely you can take a holiday when you want to?'

'Perhaps a day now and then. I could manage to be free for a day or so. If you stayed here we could spend a few hours at the cottage.'

'But there's nothing to do there and no one to talk to—only Mrs Willett.'

He had wanted to tell her that if they loved each other there would be plenty to talk about, just the two of them: their wedding and their future together, and the delight of just being together.

He had said mildly, 'Go and enjoy yourself, Sybil. Tuscany should be lovely at this time of year.'

And so Sybil had gone, with a case of new clothes and a rather careless goodbye, confident that James would be waiting for her when she came home, placid and tolerant of her demands upon his time.

He went early to the hospital on Bank Holiday Monday, and then, with the rest of the day free, went back to tell Jolly that he wouldn't be home until the late evening.

He drove first to the cottage, where he persuaded Mrs Willett to put on her hat and spend the day with him. George was to come with them, of course, and the three of them set out in the best of spirits.

Mrs Willett asked, 'Are we going somewhere nice?'

She peered at the Professor, in a sweater and casual trousers and looking years younger.

'Remember I told you of that charming family who were so kind to Sybil and me in that freak snowstorm? And the baby who was so ill? A ward sister was telling me about a children's fête to be held in the village where he lives. An old tradition, his mother told her, especially held for them on May Day. I thought we might go and have a look.'

Nanny straightened the hat which George

had inadvertently nudged to one side as he poked his head between them. 'That sounds nice,' she said placidly, and wondered what Master James was up to. He had mentioned, very briefly, the girl who had collected eggs from the hen house he had freed from the snow.

Nanny, who couldn't abide Sybil, allowed herself a few hopeful thoughts.

Nether Ditchling was *en fête* and since it was a fine day there was a good deal of activity in the street as well as the village hall. Mrs Salter had put a table outside her shop, laden with bottles of fizzy lemonade and pastries, hoping to catch any passing trade, and there were balloons hanging from all the windows. The street was filled with children being coaxed into order for the fancy dress parade, and coaxing them was Philly.

The Professor, edging the Bentley into the Vicarage gateway, saw her at once, already a bit untidy, patiently and cheerfully creating order out of chaos. He watched her, smiling, and Nanny watched him. So this was the girl.

Nothing to look at, but a happy laughing face and pretty hair, and a nicely rounded shape under that cotton dress.

'Now this is what I call a nice day out,' said Nanny, and James, his eyes on Philly, continued to smile. 'Shall we have a look?'

Philly came to meet them. 'How lovely to see you.' She beamed up at the Professor. 'Have you a day off? Mother and Father will be so pleased…'

'This is Mrs Willett, a family friend and my housekeeper.'

Philly shook hands, still beaming, and said, 'How do you do? It's a bit of a muddle at the moment—the children are getting ready for their parade. Then everyone goes to the village hall. Would you prefer to sit down somewhere quiet? Mrs Salter at the shop won't mind a bit if you have a chair in her window.'

'I'll stay here and have a good view.' Nanny, not given to easy smiling, smiled now.

Philly had bent to stroke George's head, suddenly shy because she had greeted the Professor too warmly. 'Is he your dog?' she asked, not looking higher than the Professor's chin.

'Yes. He lives at the cottage with Mrs Willett.'

'Oh, I thought you lived in London.'

'I escape to the cottage whenever I get the chance.'

He stood looking down at her, half smiling, and after a moment she said, 'I must go and sort out the children. If I see Father I'll tell him you are here.'

She slipped away and was lost in the melee of excited children.

The Professor ushered Nanny and George across the street, and Mrs Selby, coming from the village hall, saw them.

'Well,' she said, 'this is a lovely surprise.' She looked round. 'Is Miss West with you?'

'I'm afraid not. This is Mrs Willett, family friend and housekeeper, and this—' indicating placid George '—is my dog. We had a fancy to come and see you.'

'How delightful. I'll find Philly…'

'We have already met. We have been told to watch the fancy dress parade.'

'Some of us older ones are having coffee outside the shop. May I take Mrs Willett with me? We can have a cup of coffee together and watch the children at the same time. If you go to the village hall—' Mrs Selby nodded over her shoulder '—you'll find the Vicar there, arranging cakes on plates.' She added, 'The rest of the girls are here somewhere, and they will all be in the hall presently, to help with the amusements and the food.'

She took Nanny with her, and the Professor strolled along the crowded narrow pavement and into the village hall. The Vicar, with a handful of ladies to help him, was piling cakes and sandwiches on plates and stacking cups and saucers. He looked up as the Professor went in.

'This is a delightful surprise! Yes, yes, do bring your dog in. Is Miss West with you? You're on your way to Netherby, perhaps?'

'No, no. Sybil isn't with me. I've brought my housekeeper and George. We all fancied some fresh country air.'

'There's plenty of that. But isn't it coals to

Newcastle? I understand that you're a paediatrician.'

The Professor laughed. 'I like children, especially when they're happy and bursting with good health. Can I do anything to help you?'

'No, no. Indeed, you give me a good reason to leave these good ladies to finish getting everything ready.'

He led the way out of the hall and the two of them leaned against the churchyard wall and watched the children marching through the village while the grown-ups on the pavements clapped and cheered. Prizes were given at the end, of course, with the Lord of the Manor handing out picture books, paintboxes and boxes of sweets. Everyone had a consolation prize too, so that it all took some time, and the Professor, listening to the Vicar's gentle conversation, didn't take his eyes off Philly. She was oblivious of his gaze, darting here and there, blowing noses, adjusting wobbly headgear, dealing firmly with belligerent little boys who were finding the whole thing was taking too long.

Finally everyone began to make their way to the village hall, and Mrs Selby reminded the Vicar that he had promised to man the tea urn.

The Professor unfolded his great length. 'Perhaps there is something I can do? I see that Mrs Willett is happily engaged with some ladies.'

'Someone she knew years ago; they're so pleased to meet again. If you really would like to help would you mind the bran-tub? Mrs Salter's son had promised to do it, but he's just phoned to say that he's missed the train…'

So the Professor folded himself up again, onto a wooden stool, and helped small eager hands poke the sawdust in the tub in the hope of finding something they really wanted. This entailed a good deal of surreptitious feeling of the parcels in the tub, and their return when not wanted.

'You're cheating,' said Philly, and put a hand on his shoulder when he would have stood up.

'But in such a good cause. I had no idea I was so good at it!'

'Ben, our milkman, will be coming to relieve you so you can have a drink and something to

eat. Rose and Katie are making more sandwiches, but there's cheese and pickles and rolls
and beer.'

'Perfect. Are you going to keep me company?'

'Well, on and off I can. Almost everyone is
busy eating and drinking for a little while,
before the games start.' She looked up at him.
'There's a tug-o'-war; they could use you
against the farmers.'

The Professor, who would willingly have
walked on hot coals to please her, assured her
that there was nothing he'd like better. 'But
first that beer. There's nothing like a bran-tub
to give one a thirst.'

Nanny, sitting with a group of older ladies,
took an active part in their conversation while
at the same time managing to keep her eyes on
the Professor and Philly. Very happy together,
she could see that, but in a strictly friendly
way. Yet when their eyes met they smiled
together for all the world as though they were
the only two people there…

I always knew that Sybil wasn't for him, reflected Nanny, deeply satisfied.

By late afternoon people were beginning to go home, to get supper and put tired children to bed. The day had been a great success, observed the Vicar, bidding people from the Manor goodbye and then walking with the Professor to his car.

'I'm sorry you are not able to stay for supper; it would have been a pleasant ending to the day.' He shook hands and bade Nanny goodbye, then stood patiently while his wife and all five daughters made a more prolonged leavetaking. The Professor's goodbye to Philly was brief, but only she saw the look in his eyes as he glanced down at her.

It was as Mrs Selby dished out second helpings of macaroni cheese later that Katie looked across the table at Philly. 'Professor Forsyth is sweet on you, Philly. Even if he's going to marry that awful Sybil. Aren't you a lucky girl? I wouldn't mind being in your shoes…'

Philly got up from the table. 'I'll see to the hens,' she said. She left her half-empty plate and had gone before anyone could speak.

CHAPTER FOUR

THERE was a moment's silence, then everyone spoke at once. Mrs Selby hushed them. 'Katie, we all know that you didn't mean to upset Philly. She regards the Professor as a friend. Remember that he is to marry Sybil—she hasn't had much opportunity to meet people—men—as you and your sisters have had, and I'm quite sure that she thinks of him as a friend and nothing more. She's a sensible girl, long past teenage daydreams.' Of course Mrs Selby was wrong there. 'But you did embarrass her, making a joke of a casual acquaintance whom she will probably never see again.'

'I'm sorry,' burst out Katie. 'I was only teasing her a bit. And he did stare at her a lot, and when she's with him she sort of lights up...'

The Vicar said thoughtfully, 'I'm afraid that we've taken Philly for granted. Perhaps we can arrange for her to meet more people— young people. I am ashamed to own that I have always thought that Philly was content to stay here in the village, but of course she needs young society—which she would have if she had a job and met other people.'

He looked round the table. 'You all agree with me, I'm sure.'

There was a chorus of assent. 'If she could just go away and stay with someone?' suggested Rose. 'It doesn't have to be a job; she would hate that after village life. Don't we know anyone she could visit?'

After several minutes' cogitating they had to admit that there wasn't anyone. True, there was Aunt Dora, who lived in Balham, but she was in her seventies, deaf, and unlikely to know anyone younger than sixty. Then there was Cousin Maud, recently widowed and un-sociable by nature—even more so now. That left Cousin Elizabeth, quite young still, never in a job for more than a few months and boasting a host of unsuitable friends. Besides, she had only last week written to the Vicar and asked him to lend her five hundred pounds. This was an impossibility, for the heavy snow in March had damaged the roof and Noakes, the builder, had shaken his head over it and sent an estimate which precluded lending a farthing to anyone…

So it was the general regretful opinion that, for the time being at least, Philly would have to stay at home.

And then, the very next day, the unexpected happened.

Mrs Selby had a letter from a friend with whom she had kept in touch since they had been at school together. After they married—she to the Vicar, Mary to a wealthy businessman—they had remained firm friends, exchanging news several times a year.

Mrs Selby opened the letter at the breakfast table and read it slowly. When she had finished she said, 'Listen to this—a letter from Mary Lovell.' She waited until they were all looking at her. 'Her daughter Susan—remember her—

a bit younger than Philly?—well, Mary's husband has to go to America on business and Mary is going with him. Susan was to have gone, too, but she has been very ill with shingles and the doctor won't allow her to go. Mary's mother is going to stay with Susan while they are away but she asks if we could spare one of you to go and stay with her for company until they return—in a few weeks, she says.' She paused to re-read the page. 'Susan isn't ill—indeed the doctor says that it will do her good to get out and about a bit. Her grandmother's too elderly...'

Mrs Selby looked round the table and exchanged speaking glances with the Vicar and four of her daughters. Philly had bent to give Casper, the family Labrador, a crust of toast and missed it, but as she sat up she found everyone looking at her. She said, 'Let Lucy go. It's half term next weekend.'

'Not long enough—and she mustn't miss school with all those exams in another month. Philly, dear...? Just for a few weeks...you like Susan.'

'What about the hens and the garden?'

'I'll do the hens,' said Katie quickly.

'And I'll keep the garden going,' said Lucy. 'I haven't the right clothes…'

'You can have my blue dress. We can make it shorter and take it in. I dare say Susan goes to the theatre and so on.'

'I'm sure your father will give you some money, dear,' said Mrs Selby comfortably. 'A nice jersey two-piece—they always look right at any time of day—and a light raincoat, perhaps.'

Katie, anxious to atone for her ill-timed joke, offered the dressing gown she had had for her birthday, a vivid silky garment which dazzled the eyes. But she was almost the same size as Philly, and Philly, understanding why it was being offered, accepted it with gratitude.

She didn't particularly want to go. She had visited Susan and her mother once or twice over the years, but although they had been kindness itself she had missed village life and the more or less peaceful day-to-day routine. Obviously there was no one else available. And she would be back before spring slipped into summer.

'All right, I'll go,' said Philly. 'You're sure it's only for a week or two?'

'I'll ring and make sure about that.' Mrs Selby re-read the letter. 'Mary says that they will fetch you in the car next Tuesday. Goodness, I had better phone her, and then we must go shopping.' She looked at the Vicar. 'If we might have the car for an hour or two Philly can drive us—Shepton Mallett or Yeovil or Sherborne…'

So Philly found herself on the following Tuesday, sitting beside Mr Lovell in his Jaguar car, listening to his rather loud voice explaining that he wasn't sure how long he would be in the USA— 'But certainly not more than three weeks,' he told her, laughing heartily. 'We can't leave Susan for longer than that time. Her grandmother won't be much company for her.' He added hastily, 'Of course she will have you…'

Philly wasn't sure whether that was meant as a compliment or not.

The Lovells had a large Victorian house in Fulham in a prosperous-looking street obviously lived in by people of substance. As Philly got out of the car she felt sure that a maid would answer the door, not a modern version in a pinny, but one wearing a uniform and a white apron.

She was right. An elderly silent woman, in a black dress and a small white apron, opened the door to them, acknowledged Mr Lovell's greeting with a slight movement of the lips and gave Philly a quick appraising look. Philly smiled at her, which was a waste of time. London, thought Philly. Everyone's a stranger.

Mrs Lovell welcomed her warmly, though, and Susan was glad to see her. Grandmother Lovell, sitting in a high-backed chair with her feet on a stool, offered a hand and observed in a dry old voice that she hoped that Philly would enjoy her stay. 'I must depend upon you to keep Susan amused.'

Which remark made Philly wish that she was back at home.

It took her only a few days to discover that Susan's grandmother wanted nothing to do with Susan's activities—indeed they saw very little of her, since she breakfasted in bed and they were almost always out for lunch. Only in the evenings did they dine together, and then the old lady talked a great deal about herself and her youth and evinced no desire to know what they had been doing all day.

Philly might miss village life, but there was a lot to be said for London's attractions. There were the shops; Susan, with plenty of money to spend, would spend the morning at Harrods, poring over the cosmetics counter or trying on clothes. 'Mother and Father like me to look smart,' she explained complacently to Philly. She cast a not unkind look at Philly's knitted two-piece. 'Of course you don't need to have a lot of clothes, do you? Don't you ever want to live here in London?'

Philly said that no, she didn't, but added politely that she was enjoying her visit. 'There's so much to see—the shops and the parks and seeing the Horse Guards riding...' She hesitated. 'Do you ever visit any of the museums?'

'Well, only if Mother and Father have been

invited to something special at one of them. Did you want to go to one? I tell you what, there's an exhibition of Chinese porcelain—I can't remember where, but we can easily find out… I don't mind going—it's the fashionable thing to do. We might even get our photos in one of the society magazines.'

'I'd like that,' said Philly. She didn't know anything about Chinese porcelain but she was willing to learn, although she didn't like the idea of having her photo in the papers. It was not very likely, she told herself. Hers was the kind of face that people passed over without even seeing it.

Susan was as good as her word. She was not a clever girl, and was too lazy to do anything about it, but she was kind and she liked Philly and felt vaguely sorry for her since she lived buried in the country and had no fun. It puzzled Susan that she seemed content to dwindle into middle age without even the prospect of marrying. Susan, at twenty-three, thought of thirty as being the end of youth and beauty, and Philly was twenty-seven, although she didn't seem to mind in the least.

It was a fine morning; it would have to be the knitted two-piece again. The saleswoman who had sold it to her had commented that it was a well-bred outfit, suitable for any occasion. Philly, looking around her once they were in the museum, hoped that she was right. At least it was so unassuming that it passed unnoticed amongst the elegant outfits surrounding her.

The porcelain was magnificent. Philly forgot about everything else and went slowly from one showcase to the next, reading all the little tickets and trying to appreciate what she read. They had been there about half an hour when Susan nudged her. 'I've seen some friends of mine over there. Do you mind if I go and talk to them?'

Philly, bent double over a fragile dish in its own glass case, nodded absently, to be brought upright by a voice behind her.

'The last person I would have expected to see here.'

Sybil West, the picture of elegance, was smiling at her as she stood up.

'Surely this isn't quite your scene?' went on Sybil, and turned to smile at the woman with her. 'My dear, imagine! This is the Vicar's daughter—the one with the sausages.'

They both laughed, but Philly, red in the face, nonetheless said politely, 'Hello, Miss West. I'm surprised at meeting you here, too. But life's full of surprises, isn't it?'

'Pleasant ones, too.'

Philly turned round smartly. The Professor was standing there. There was nothing in his face to tell her whether he had heard their brief exchange. He smiled down at her and then he nodded at Sybil. 'Sorry, I couldn't get here earlier—and I can't stay. I'm afraid I'll have to break our date for this evening.'

Sybil said angrily, 'That's the second time this week…'

Philly edged away. The woman who had been with Sybil had already turned her back to talk to someone else, but the Professor's hand was suddenly on her arm.

'You're not on your own?'

'No. With a friend.'

'You're staying in London?'

'Yes.' Philly was very conscious of the hand, so she smiled at Sybil. 'It was nice meeting you again. I must find my friend. Goodbye.'

She looked at the Professor and then wished him goodbye, too, in a stiff little voice, and met his eyes for a brief moment. He dropped his hand from her arm and she slipped away to lose herself in the crowd.

When she found Susan she was forced to explain who the tall good-looking man was. 'I saw him talking to you, but I didn't dare interrupt. Who is he? Someone important? And there was a girl with you, too. She looked cross.'

So Philly explained sufficiently to satisfy Susan's curiosity.

'A pity—I thought just for a moment that he was keen on you, Philly.'

She laughed, and Philly laughed with her, and wished that she was back home where she would be able to forget Professor Forsyth and the way he had looked at her.

Wishful thinking, reflected Philly, never did anyone any good.

When they left the museum a few minutes later the Professor was at the door, talking to the porter, and what was more natural than that he should speak to Philly?

'Are you staying long in London?' he asked her and looked at Susan.

'Just for a week or two, to keep Susan company. Susan, this is Professor Forsyth. Susan Lovell—Professor Forsyth.'

They shook hands and Susan, as she would tell her mother later, had the instant and urgent feeling that Philly and this professor wanted to be alone. A girl of impulses, she didn't hesitate.

'Philly, I've just remembered. I promised Granny that if I saw Lady Savill here I would ask her about the bridge party. And she is here. I must go back and talk to her, and she'll be so long-winded she might even invite me to lunch. You go on back and tell Granny, will you? Get a ninety-three bus.'

She had gone before Philly could speak.

'I'm going the same way as the ninety-three bus,' said the Professor, deceptively casual. 'I'll give you a lift.'

'Really? You wouldn't mind? I'm not quite sure about the buses. Susan lives in Fulham—if you're going that way?'

He assured her that he was and led the way to the car. Fulham wasn't all that distance, but the lunch hour traffic was building up and he had no intention of taking the quickest route. Philly was constantly in his thoughts and now she was here with him, sitting beside him, answering his carefully casual questions with all the openness of a child.

London, she told him, was very interesting, and parts of it were really very pleasant. 'But some of the side streets look very depressing. Rows and rows of little brick houses with no gardens. I do hope that the people who live in them go for holidays to the sea or to the country…'

'I think a good many of them do.' The Professor turned down a side street which would lengthen their drive considerably. 'But you would be surprised to know how many of them dislike the country, even for a holiday—country such as Nether Ditchling, with no shops or cinemas or amusement arcades. You see, they don't need to walk for miles to get eggs; everything is on the doorstep or at the supermarket.' He glanced at her. 'Mrs Salter's shop is hardly a fair exchange to them.'

'Well, yes, I dare say Nether Ditchling is a bit dull...'

'But you wouldn't wish to leave it?'

'I'm very happy there.' She didn't say more, thinking wistfully that she would leave the village and go to the ends of the earth if he asked her to.

They were nearing their journey's end.

'Do you know where we are?'

'Yes. It's the second road on the left and then the first road on the right,' said Philly. She added, 'It was lovely to see you again. I didn't think we would—I mean, you living here and being important and me living at home.'

As he drew up before the house which she had pointed out she asked, 'When are you getting married?' She had her hand on the door and he got out to open it for her. On the pavement she added, looking up at his calm face, 'You mustn't marry her; she'll make you very unhappy.'

The street door had been opened by the severe maid and Philly skipped up the steps and into the house, so appalled at what she had said that she forgot to say goodbye or thank you.

She avoided the maid's astonished stare and ran upstairs to her room. Her tongue had run away with her with a vengeance, and the faint hope that the Professor might not have heard her wasn't worth a second thought. Would it be best to write and apologise? Or ignore the whole regrettable happening? She stared at her face in the mirror and wished that she was at home; that today was still yesterday, that she had never gone to the museum…

She went downstairs to join Susan's granny in the sitting room and give an account of her morning. She explained why Susan had gone back to talk to Lady Savill, and then listened politely to the old lady's long-winded account of her friendship with her.

Philly, listening with half an ear, was startled when she was suddenly asked sharply why she wasn't married or at least engaged.

'I don't know,' she said. 'No one has ever asked me…'

'You have never met a man whom you wish to marry?'

Philly went a bright pink. Incurably honest, she said, 'Oh, yes, but he doesn't know.'

'There are ways of letting a man know,' said Granny Lovell, 'and you're no fool.'

'That isn't possible. There are circumstances…'

'In that case you must hope that fate will intervene, as she so often does.' Granny Lovell heaved herself up against her cushions. 'Pour me another glass of sherry, child.'

Philly, reflecting that elderly grannies should never be written off as dim old ladies, filled her glass obediently.

Susan came back then, with messages from Lady Savill.

'Did you get a bus? You knew where to get off?'

'Well, Professor Forsyth said he was coming this way so he gave me a lift.'

'I thought perhaps he would. He looked nice. Known him long, Philly?'

'And who is this professor?' asked Granny, and fixed Philly with a beady eye not to be ignored.

'Well,' began Philly, 'he's not really a friend, only someone I met by accident, and then again when we had that snow.' She added soberly, 'He's engaged to a very beautiful girl. Susan, you saw her at the museum. You said she looked cross.'

'And so she did! Do you know her, Philly?'

'We've met several times, but only because we were both in the same place at the same time, if you see what I mean.'

'Well, she didn't look your sort,' said Susan. 'Granny, if you've finished your sherry may we have lunch? I'm simply starving.'

Going to bed that night, Philly wondered if the Professor would come to the house now that he knew where she was staying. There was no reason why he should—indeed, he had probably forgotten where she was staying by

now, and he had evinced no wish to see her
again. Remembering the way they had parted,
she conceded that it was highly unlikely that
the idea would even cross his mind.

I am behaving like an idiot, Philly told herself,
and anyway I don't want to see him ever again
after what I said. Half-asleep, she muttered, 'I'm
bewitched. The sooner I go home the better.'

The Professor was still smiling as he let
himself into his flat, and Jolly, coming to meet
him in the hall, said, 'Come up on the pools,
have you? Haven't seen you look so pleased
with yourself for a month of Sundays, sir.'

The Professor tossed his bag on a chair and
picked up his post from the console table. 'The
pools, Jolly? No, no—I have discovered
nirvana, glimpsed a future.'

He went to his study and shut the door and
Jolly went back to his kitchen.

'And what's got into him?' he asked Tabby,
his cat. 'It certainly isn't that Miss West. He's
never smiled like that for her…'

* * *

The following week the Lovells came back and Philly was driven home, clasping a tee shirt emblazoned with American slogans which she didn't think would go down well in Nether Ditchling, her ears ringing with the Lovells' thanks. Granny had bidden her goodbye in her tart manner, with the hope that she had taken advantage of her visit, which had made her feel that she was the one who should be thanking them. London had been interesting, she admitted, but the only reason she would wish to return there was because Professor Forsyth lived and worked there. But that was a thought she kept to herself.

It was lovely to be home again. She gave the tee shirt to Lucy, who had been looking after the hens for her, and then handed round the small presents she had bought and gave a detailed account of the pleasures she had had, the places she had been to and the shops she had visited.

'But everyone's in a hurry,' she explained. 'Going somewhere or coming back from somewhere…'

'So you wouldn't want to live there?' observed her father.

'Only if I had a very good reason, Father. I am very happy to be home again.'

Something in her voice made her mother look at her sharply. Perhaps she had met someone—a man—while she was in London. But Philly was a grown woman, not a young daughter to be questioned...

The Professor, meanwhile, was in his study working. But after half an hour or so of writing, he sat back in his chair and allowed his thoughts free rein. He allowed his thoughts to dwell pleasurably on Philly until they were interrupted by the phone. It was Sybil...

A friend of hers had told her with concealed spite that James had been seen talking alone with that funny little creature who had been at the museum. What was more, the friend had added, he had put her in his car and driven off— 'They seemed to know each other very well...'

'Someone we both know,' Sybil had said sweetly. 'A girl we met earlier this year. We're both rather sorry for her. She lives in the country—a very dull life…'

'When you spoke to her in the museum you didn't sound sorry for her,' the friend had pointed out. She'd laughed. 'You'd better watch your back, darling.'

Sybil had laughed too, then, but when she had gone home she'd sat down to think.

Perhaps she was a bit too sure of James. Perhaps she had been away too much, not wanting to spend her time with him at that boring cottage. This girl might be a real danger. Sybil was shrewd enough to know that James might want something more than a glamorous companion on an evening out, and the girl was bright enough to see that. 'The stupid creature,' Sybil had hissed aloud.

But Sybil had a good deal of charm when she wished to use it, and said now, 'Darling, am I interrupting you at work? Only I wanted to tell you how glad I was that you gave Philly that lift last week. It was such a surprise to see her at the exhibition, and she wasn't a bit happy about being there. I quite forgot to ask her where she was staying—I thought I might take her out to lunch, somewhere rather chic. I don't suppose she gets out much when she's home. Have you her address?'

'Somewhere in Fulham. I didn't notice the street or the house. But she will be back home by now.'

Sybil was too clever to press the point. James sounded as calm and composed as he always did, but that wasn't to say that he wasn't intending to see Philly. She said sweetly, 'What a pity. I hope she had a good time; her friend looked rather nice. I won't keep you, darling, but I hope I'll see you at the Mastertons' dinner party. Don't work too hard!'

Sybil put down the phone and sat down to think once more. She had every intention of marrying James, but in her own good time. In the meantime, though, she must make sure that his eye didn't wander.

She had a great belief in her ability to charm him; she was lovely to look at, dressed beautifully, and hid a keen intelligence beneath effortless conversation and the ability to be amusing. She was also greedy and selfish, quick-tempered, and quite uncaring about anyone or anything which didn't concern her personally, and, knowing this, she was careful to conceal the true side of her nature. Just once or twice she had allowed it to show and she knew that James had seen it.

Philly must be made to be out of reach, but how? It seemed that she had no boyfriends, no prospect of marrying anyone at Nether Ditchling. A boyfriend must be found—better still a man who professed himself to be serious about her. She knew James well enough to know that he would accept that, whatever his own feelings were.

There must be someone who would play the part of devoted admirer. Someone who enjoyed a joke at someone else's expense and wasn't too scrupulous about hurting feelings…

And there was. Her cousin, a young tearaway with too much money and too much time on his hands. She had had a phone call from him recently, deploring his dull life while he recovered from a skiing accident.

He was, she judged, ripe for some amusement...

Wasting no time, she drove herself down to the country house in Norfolk where he was staying with his parents until he was fit enough to return to his London flat.

Her aunt and uncle, who didn't like her particularly, nevertheless welcomed her as someone who would relieve Gregory's boredom, and she had ample opportunity to spend hours with him as he limped around the gardens, grumbling, ripe for any mischief offered to him.

It would be a joke, she told him. No one would get hurt—not that either of them cared about that.

'James is getting impatient to marry,' she told him, 'and I don't want to tie myself down yet. James has everything, you know that, but we don't see eye to eye about some things. I'm still working on him, and while I'm doing that I can't have him being distracted by another woman. This girl's a walk-over, a real country miss—keeps hens and teaches Sunday School, full of good deeds. One look at you limping into the village and she's yours.'

'What's her name?'

'Philomena, believe it or not! Everyone calls her Philly. She's quite plain and wears the most awful clothes.'

'You don't suppose James has fallen for her?'

'Not for one moment. She just happened to turn up at the right moment, though. Do say that you'll help me out, Gregory. Besides, it will keep you amused while you get fit again.'

'What's in it for me?'

'A bit of fun to keep you amused, as I said, and I'll wangle an invitation to the Strangeways', on their yacht. Everyone would give their eye teeth to get asked…'

She looked sideways at him; he was a good-looking young man, and could be charming when he had his own way. And he was quite as heartless and as selfish as she was. Absolutely ideal for her plan.

'It's on,' said Gregory. 'When do I start?'

'You know the people at Netherby, don't

you? You couldn't go to the wedding because of your accident, but you're well enough acquainted with them for me to drive you down there. There should be a chance of getting a weekend invitation. Nether Ditchling is only a few miles away. You could run out of petrol, or some such thing, and contrive to get yourself into the Vicarage.'

The Professor was going to Birmingham, to the children's hospital there, in a week's time. There was ample time before that to drive to Netherby with Gregory.

It all went splendidly. The newly-weds weren't back from honeymoon and everyone was feeling a bit flat; new faces were welcome and Gregory could be charming and amusing. They were glad of a diversion, and he was invited to stay for a week or so.

Sybil drove him back to London, delighted with the success of her plan.

'I can't stay for more than a week or ten days,' observed Gregory. 'I mean, I know the family slightly, but not enough to outstay my welcome.'

'Then you'll have to put up at a pub some-where close.'

When he demurred, she said slyly, 'I met Joyce Strangeway a day or two ago—you'll get your invitation…' She went on, ignoring his pleased grin, 'There's a good pub at Wisbury; that's only about three miles from Nether Ditchling. It's only for a few weeks,' she added coaxingly, 'Just long enough for James to be told about it. I'll do that, and get him to drive me down to Nether Ditchling. You can be there, being very possessive about Philly.'

'Supposing she doesn't like me?'

'Don't be a fool, Gregory. You can make anyone like you if you choose.'

The Professor, dining with Sybil on the evening before he went to Birmingham, found her in a charming mood, ready to amuse him, prepared to listen to his infrequent references to his work, talking with smiling vagueness about their future.

In this compliant mood, he reflected,

perhaps they could talk seriously, discover if their feelings for each other were deep enough, and perhaps agree mutually to free each other from an engagement which had gone on too long and become meaningless.

But Sybil, wary of such talk, gave him no chance to start a serious conversation. When at length he said, 'Sybil, I think we should have a talk,' she pretended not to hear, but waved to friends at a nearby table and suggested that they should join them for coffee.

The Professor, whose good manners prevented him from not welcoming her friends, resolved to go and see Sybil when he got back from Birmingham.

The following day Sybil drove Gregory down to Netherby House, spent a few hours there, and then drove back to town. There was nothing more she could do until James came back; her plan depended on Gregory now.

Gregory was the perfect guest when he exerted himself. On the third day of his visit he proposed talking himself off for the day— 'So that you won't get too tired of me around the house,' he told his hostess.

When she protested about his lame leg he told her that he could drive quite easily in his small sports car, and besides, there was almost no traffic.

He set off after breakfast, saying that he might drive down to the coast and wouldn't be back before the late afternoon, and then he idled his way to Nether Ditchling, a half-formed plan in his head. He drove into the village slowly and stopped at Mrs Salter's shop. He went inside, exaggerating his limp, aware that it aroused friendly sympathy. He wished her a sunny good morning and bought a newspaper, and then took the local paper as well.

'Haven't seen you before,' observed Mrs Salter. 'Touring, are you?'

'Hardly that. I'm looking for somewhere to live. I've been told that there are several places for sale in this part of the country.'

It was a shot in the dark that found its mark.

'Well, now,' said Mrs Salter, delighted to have a good gossip. 'You're right there. There's Appletrees at the end of the village. Nice little place—a bit pokey though, if you have young children.'

Gregory smiled. 'I'm not married yet, but I'd want a place where there was plenty of room.'

'Well, there's Old Thatch, between here and Wisbury, and the Old Manor, a mile or so from this end of the village. Nice place with a good big garden.'

'That sounds just right. There's an agent?'

He couldn't believe his luck when Mrs Salter said, 'Mr Selby, the Vicar, has the keys. It's a bit out of the way and the agent has to come a long way. Besides, no one has been to see it for months.'

Gregory gave her a winning smile. 'It may be just what I'm looking for. Bless you for telling me about it. Where is the Vicarage?'

Mrs Salter beamed. 'See the church? It's that redbrick house just beyond it. The Vicar will take you round the Old Manor. He's a very nice gentleman.'

Gregory smiled again. 'I hope we shall meet again,' he told her, and went back to his car. This was going to be his day…!

CHAPTER FIVE

THE Vicarage door was open. Gregory pulled the old-fashioned bell and listened to the distant sound of voices and then hurrying feet. The girl who opened the door wider had to be Philly—Sybil's description of her had been accurate and, he had to admit, spiteful. No looks, but a lovely smile, a mouth which turned up at the corners and beautiful eyes. And her friendly, 'Good morning,' was uttered in a soft voice.

For a moment Gregory felt mean, but then he remembered the Strangeways' yacht, and he returned Philly's smile.

'Good morning. I do apologise for bothering you, but Mrs Salter told me that perhaps the Vicar could help me.'

'Come in. I'll fetch him for you.' She

ushered him into the drawing room. 'Do sit down. Father won't be a minute.'

Gregory sat, but got up as soon as she had left him. The room was large and the furniture in it was good solid stuff, worth quite a bit. There were some good pictures on the walls too, although the armchairs and the sofa were shabby. He went to the window and looked out, then turned round as the door opened and the Vicar came in.

Gregory smiled his charming smile. 'Good morning, Sir. I hope I'm not disturbing you, but Mrs Salter at the shop sent me to you. I'm looking for a house and she was telling me about the Old Manor and that you had the keys. I should very much like to look over it at your convenience. If you would suggest a time?'

A polite young man and I don't like him. I wonder why? thought the Vicar.

'Why not now? I am free for an hour or so, and it is only a couple of miles from here. Do you have a car?'

'Yes, I'm staying at Netherby House for a

week or so.' Gregory held out a hand. 'Gregory Finch.'

The Vicar shook hands. 'Then let us go at once. I'll get the keys. The house has been empty for some time. It's a delightful place, but needs some refurbishment.'

He went away for the keys, and they were going down the path to the car when Philly called from the door. 'Father, the Armstrongs have phoned. Mr Armstrong's worse; they ask if you'd go right away...'

'Of course.' The Vicar turned back to the house. 'You must forgive me. An elderly parishioner, gravely ill. I must ask you to come at some other time.'

Philly had joined them. 'I'll take this gentleman, Father. Now he's here he might just as well have a look at the house. He can come back if he likes it and discuss it with you. It's the Old Manor, isn't it? I saw you take the keys...'

'Very well, my dear. Lock up well, won't you? I may possibly be back within an hour or so, and Mr Finch is welcome to wait here if he wishes to know more about the house.'

He hurried into the street and Philly said, 'Will you wait a minute while I tell Mother?' and she went back into the house.

Mrs Selby had been looking at them from the drawing-room window. A good-looking young man, she considered, obviously recovering from some injury to his leg. She turned her attention to the sports car, and as Philly came in she said, 'He looks all right, but don't let him drive too fast.'

Gregory, seeing her watching him from the window, exaggerated the limp. Older ladies, he had discovered, had a soft spot for the lame.

He was careful to be politely formal with Philly as they drove the short distance to the Old Manor, and once there he inspected the place slowly, asking all the right questions, discussing the garden at some length, asking about the neighbourhood and the village.

'It is delightful,' he told her. 'I should very much like to come again and inspect the place more thoroughly. When is it most convenient for me to come?'

'Well, Saturday afternoons are mostly free

for Father, or any time on Monday. He might be called away, of course…'

He stood aside politely while she locked the house door. 'Then if I come on Monday around eleven o'clock? I can wait if the Vicar is engaged. I'm able to please myself until my leg is quite fit again and I shall enjoy looking round the church and the village.'

He gave her a quick look and saw that he was behaving exactly as she would expect him to behave.

Philly nodded. 'If you don't mind having to wait Mother will be glad to give you coffee. You won't want to walk too far with that leg.'

Back at the Vicarage they found that the Vicar was still away. Mrs Selby offered coffee and suggested that Gregory might like to wait, but he was satisfied with his morning's work. He mustn't rush things. Certainly he must phone Sybil. He thanked her, got into his car and drove away.

'Was he interested?' asked Mrs Selby.

'He seemed to be. He didn't say much but he

wants to go again and talk to Father about it. He was very polite…'

Mrs Selby agreed, ignoring the vague thought that she didn't like him.

Gregory had said that he must drive back to Netherby for lunch, but he had no intention of doing so; he had told his hostess that he would be away all day and he intended to drive to Bath.

He had had enough of the country already, and a civilised pub and a decent restaurant would help him to while away the hours. He hoped that Sybil's plan could be carried out quickly, before he got too bored. He pulled into a lay-by and dialled her number on his mobile phone. She would probably not be home…

But she was, and avid to hear if he had been able to meet Philly.

He told her, and listened to her delighted praise. 'Gregory, you're a marvel. Now I must get James to go to Nether Ditchling and you must manage to be there… I'll phone you as soon as I know something. What did you think of Philly?'

'I don't know why you're making such a

fuss, Sybil.' When she made an impatient sound, he said, 'Oh, all right, I'll help you out. It will give me something to do in all this boring country, and it shouldn't be too hard to fix up something. I'm already on good terms with the Vicar and his wife, and it'll be amusing to get Philly interested in me.'

'I knew you'd help me,' said Sybil, and added cunningly, 'I met David Smale yesterday; he's been invited by the Strangeways to join them on their yacht. He had heard that you had been invited too.'

Gregory smiled to himself. 'Let me know what you plan to do and give me as much warning as you can.'

It seemed as though the fates were on Sybil's side. A carefully casual wish that James might drive her to Netherby so that she could see Coralie met with willing agreement.

He would be free on Saturday. They could have lunch on the way and get to Netherby in the early afternoon, he suggested. Perhaps if he and Sybil saw more of each other—and she had been very sweet and undemanding lately—they could talk about their future. Their separate futures. Her vagueness about it forced him to think that she had no wish to settle down to married life, with a husband and children, and if she would admit that, then they could part amicably with no hard feelings.

He told Jolly that he would be driving Miss West to Netherby on Saturday afternoon, looking so pleased about it that Jolly went to his kitchen and brooded over a future dominated by that lady.

But the Professor was looking pleased because there was a good chance that he might see Philly as they drove through Nether Ditchling.

Which, of course he would.

Gregory couldn't believe his luck. Primed by Sybil that she and James should be at the village around two o'clock, he had had no difficulty in asking the Vicar to arrange for him to see the Old Manor again. There was the chance that something would upset their timetable, but he thought it unlikely. They both had their phones; Sybil could ring him when they stopped for lunch and give him a good idea at about what time they should reach Nether Ditchling.

He made his own plans and spent the best part of the morning playing the dutiful guest.

'Such a charming young man,' observed his hostess. 'So thoughtful and so amusing. I shall miss him when he goes.'

Her husband, in the habit of keeping his own opinions to himself, grunted in a non-committal manner which allowed her to think that he agreed with her.

Saturday was a busy day for Philly: typing her father's sermon, since he could never read his own notes, making up beds for Rose's and Flora's fiancés, picking the broad beans for Sunday lunch, going to do the church flowers with whichever of the village ladies whose turn it was.

It was warm for the time of year. 'Likely it's

a taste of 'an 'ot summer,' the milkman had said early that morning, a remark which had encouraged Philly to put on a cotton blouse and a denim skirt before going to lay the table for lunch.

Her mother and father, Katie and Lucy and herself would be there. It was to be omelettes and a salad, with rolls warm from Mr Brisk's bakery in the next village.

They all had a great deal to say over their simple meal, for they liked to talk, airing their views, encouraged by the Vicar, who found small talk a waste of time, so that it was later than usual when they got up from the table.

'What time is Mr Finch coming?' asked Katie.

Mrs Selby looked at the clock. 'Goodness, it's almost two o'clock. He said between two and half past…'

But there was no sign of him when Katie went to look.

They washed up and put the tea tray ready, and Philly went to the hen house to cast an eye over a broody hen. By that time it was almost half past two.

* * *

As James slowed the Bentley when they reached the village Gregory slid to a halt outside the Vicarage. Things couldn't be better; now it was up to Sybil…

She had seen him; she put an urgent hand on James' sleeve. 'Stop, James, do stop. That's my cousin by the Vicarage gate—remember I told you he was staying at Netherby? I must say hello.'

They greeted each other as though they hadn't seen each other for months. Sybil introduced the men and asked, 'Whatever are you doing here, Gregory?'

'Waiting for Philly,' he told her with a smile. 'I'm driving her to Bath to do some shopping. Of course—you know her?' His glance swept from Sybil to the Professor. 'We met over at Netherby and we rather fell for each other.' The lies tripped off his tongue with easy assurance. 'Forgive me if I don't stay talking; I'd better see if she is ready.'

He got out of his car and started up the Vicarage path with an airy wave of the hand. Of course if the Vicar or his wife were to come out now he would be in an awkward spot…but no one came. He turned at the door and waved again, and saw the Bentley slip away.

He spent a tedious afternoon with the Vicar, inspecting drains and walls and discussing the need for roof repairs, and towards the end of the afternoon his mobile phone rang.

It was Sybil, phoning from Netherby, and he said at once, 'You're in town? This evening? May I phone you back?' He glanced at the Vicar and said, 'An old friend in town for a couple of days. Wants me to meet him for dinner.'

'Well, I think you have inspected this house very thoroughly. Suppose we go back to the Vicarage and have a cup of tea and you can drive to town from there? You will want to warn them at Netherby…'

Gregory hid a grin. Everything was going splendidly. 'I'll phone them now.'

'I'll go and turn the car and start locking up,' said the Vicar, and wandered off.

Gregory dialled and said loudly, 'It's Gregory. Would you forgive me if I go straight to town?' and then softly, once the Vicar was out of the room, 'Sybil, we're just leaving; I'm having tea at the Vicarage. Any chance of you getting there? There's nothing to stop you knocking on the door and paying a friendly visit. Bring the Professor with you, of course, and I'll do my stuff with Philly.'

He heard her delighted giggle. 'I can't promise anything, but I'll do my best.'

It wasn't difficult to suggest getting back to London. Sybil made her excuses in her charming way, and in the car again she said coaxingly, 'You don't mind, darling? I do love the country, but after an hour or so I've had enough. We can get tea on the way. Where shall we go this evening?'

'We'll stop for tea, but I'm speaking at a dinner this evening…'

'Tomorrow we could go to Henley—go on the river.' When he hesitated, she said, 'Oh, all right, you don't want to go. You never do what I want to do, do you? But you expect me to trail down to that cottage of yours and be bored to tears.'

It seemed as good a time as any. The Professor said quietly, 'We must talk, Sybil…'

They were nearing the Vicarage and she shouted, 'Well, I don't want to talk. Stop—I want a cup of tea and I'm going to the Vicarage. After all, they seem to keep open house.'

'We can have tea further along the road. You can't interrupt their afternoon.'

She pointed her finger at Gregory's car. 'Why not? It looks as though Gregory has.'

Against his better judgement, the Professor stopped the car. Sybil flounced out and up the path to the Vicarage door, half-open as usual. Since they were having tea in the drawing room the entire Selby family saw her—and the Professor coming more slowly.

Mrs Selby got up and went to meet Sybil. 'Just in time for tea,' she said kindly. 'And your cousin is here on his way up to London. Come in. I think you know nearly everyone here.' She turned to smile at the Professor. 'This is a delightful surprise. The girls are always asking when they will see you again.'

'This is an intrusion, Mrs Selby.'

'Nonsense. We love visitors, especially un-expected ones.'

Sybil was already sitting by the Vicar, being offered tea and cake, and in the general upheaval Gregory took care to sit next to Philly, joining in the general talk and at the same time contriving to pay her special atten-tion.

Philly, being polite by nature, smiled at his joking description of getting lost, and answered him when he asked her something, speaking in a low voice which the Professor was quick to note. He made civil conversation with the Vicar and stifled the desire to wring Gregory's neck and then Philly's.

Mrs Selby, apparently unobservant, said quietly, 'Philly, fill the teapot, will you, dear? You'll need more tea.' And, after a few moments, 'James—I may call you James?—would you go to the kitchen and tell Philly to bring the other cake? It's in the cupboard by the Aga.'

Philly was sitting on the kitchen table, swinging her legs and watching the kettle boil.

Part of her felt happy, for the Professor was here in the house and she hadn't expected that, and part of her was unhappy because Sybil looked so beautiful and so sure of herself, glancing at him from time to time and smiling. She wasn't surprised that he was in love with her...

He walked in and stood in front of her. 'Your mother wants the other cake. Did you have a pleasant afternoon...?'

'Oh, yes. We went walking; it's so nice being with someone you like, isn't it?' Indeed it had been nice; she hadn't seen Mrs Twist's elderly father for some time, and there had been such a lot to talk about now that Baby Twist was once more a bouncing infant, the apple of his grandfather's eye. She went on, wishing that he didn't look so cross, 'He's staying here for a week or two, so we shall see each other quite often. He doesn't care for London and he's looking for somewhere to live round here.'

The Professor glowered and said, 'Indeed?' in a voice to freeze any attempt at light conversation.

It was a good thing that the kettle boiled just

then. She made fresh tea and fetched the cake and gave it to him to carry.

Sybil gave them a sharp glance as they went back into the drawing room and a few moments later got up to go.

'We're going out this evening,' she said, and apologised prettily for leaving so quickly, waiting with ill-concealed impatience as James made his more leisurely farewells.

When they had gone Mrs Selby said, 'What a beautiful young woman she is,' and everyone agreed, although Katie, remembering how upset Philly had been when she had voiced her opinion once before, held her tongue.

Sybil broke the silence in the car. 'What a nice family—and the girls are so pretty. Not Philly, of course, although she's quite sweet. And what a surprise to find Gregory almost one of the family. They certainly seemed on excellent terms, he and Philly. It's time he settled down.'

'Aren't you being rather premature?' James spoke casually, but, glancing at his profile, Sybil noted its grimness.

'Perhaps, but you must admit that Philly looked happy.'

'How long is Gregory staying at Netherby? He's going up to town this evening, isn't he?'

'He's meeting a friend for dinner…'

'Does he work?'

'Oh, yes. Something in the City. But he's got leave until his leg is quite better. He has money of his own, of course. My uncle's got a small estate in Norfolk.'

All of this was said with an air of such honesty, yet somehow the Professor's handsome nose smelled a rat…

With only vague plans made for a future meeting, he dropped Sybil off and drove to his flat, where Jolly took one look at his face and retired discreetly to the kitchen.

'In a mood,' he told his cat. 'Best leave him for a bit and then dish up something tasty. No doubt that Miss West's been upsetting him again.'

The Professor wasn't upset, he was in a towering rage. He had taken an instant dislike to Gregory, and to his air of possessiveness each time he looked at or spoke to Philly. If he had been a decent fellow, James told himself, he would have accepted the situation, but Gregory was the very last man for Philly. Besides, he wasn't sure that she liked him, let alone loved him…

He went in search of Jolly presently. 'I'm going down to the cottage tomorrow. Have the day off—I'll not be back until early evening.'

'I thought that was what you might be doing. There's a marrow bone in the fridge for George.'

Mrs Willett was delighted when he phoned her. 'There'll be roast pork and apple sauce, and one of my treacle tarts, and we can have a good gossip.' Which meant that she would ask innumerable questions without once probing his private life, knowing that if he wished to he would tell her anything he wanted to.

She knew that he was a very reserved man— he had many friends, but they knew very little about him other than his work. Not one of them approved of Sybil, but they liked him too much to say so, even in the vaguest way.

Mrs Willett didn't like her either, but she was prepared to do her best to do so if that would make her Master James a happy man.

He wasn't happy; she saw that at a glance although she said nothing. He had a problem and she hoped that he might tell her about it. And sure enough, the pork and apple sauce disposed of, the washing up done and the pair of them sitting in the garden with George at their feet, the Professor said, 'Nanny, I need your advice…'

'If I can help, I will,' said Nanny, 'and I'll listen.'

When he had finished, he added, 'You see, Nanny, I love her, and if she loves this Gregory and wants to marry him I'll not see her again. But, whether or not she does love him, I know that I cannot marry Sybil. I suppose that I should feel very much to blame for that, but I have known for some time now that she doesn't love me. She is beautiful and charming, but behind that there is nothing. And before I say goodbye to Philly I want to make sure that she will be happy. Do you know, Nanny, I think that something is not quite right about this Gregory? Though Sybil told me that his home is in Norfolk and that he has a job in the City.'

Nanny was brisk and matter-of-fact. 'Find out where this man lives and go and see where it is—perhaps manage to meet his father or family. Find out where he works, discover his friends. And don't tell me that you can't, for you know any number of people who could help you. If he's a good man and loves Philly, and you're satisfied about him, then you can bid her goodbye and take up your life again. If there's something wrong, you can put it right.'

'That is what I've been thinking. I needed someone to tell me that I wasn't behaving like a fool.'

It was a few days later, discussing a small patient's complicated fractured leg, that the Professor's colleague remarked, 'Uncommon case this. Only seen one other. A young man some months ago. Private patient and gave a good deal of trouble so I understand—chatting up the nurses, having drinks smuggled in and so on. Told me that he had an executive job in the City; turned out to be a job in name only, working in the family firm whenever her felt like it. Didn't pay his bill, either. His father settled it finally, explained that though his son had money of his own he was still sowing his wild oats.'

The Professor listened to this with an expressionless face and finally said, 'I seem to have heard about this—was it Finch…?'

'Very likely. The father has a small estate in Norfolk; not liked in the neighbourhood. I made it my business to find out before I sent in my bill.'

'I wonder why I remember the name?' observed the Professor guilelessly. 'A village not too far from the sea?' It was a lucky guess.

'That's right—inland from Great Yarmouth. Limberthorpe. A dozen houses and a church.' He glanced at his watch. 'I must go. Let me know how that leg does…'

The Professor went home and got out a road map. He would be free on Sunday. From what he had heard his dearest Philly had fallen in love with a man who would make her unhappy, but he must give the fellow the benefit of the doubt. He might not be as black as his colleague had painted, and the only way to find out was to go and see for himself. Surely someone in a village as small as Limberthorpe would let drop a hint or two.

He set off early in the morning and reached Limberthorpe in time to join the handful of men in the bar of the village pub. They paused in their talk as he went in. He ordered a pint and sat at the bar, making no attempt to join in their conversation.

Presently one of the men said, 'You're strange to these parts?'

'Just passing through. This village looked so pleasant I stopped for a while.'

"'Tis pleasant enough,' said an old man, 'for them as passes on their way.'

He paused, and the Professor recognised this

as a strong hint that a round was called for. This done, he said casually, 'Why do you say that?'

'Being sold up lock, stock and barrel, the big house. The old man wants to go and live with his daughter, and young Mr Finch he can't be bothered with the place, you see. Likes London and racketing around. Can't be bothered with the house, never been interested in the village.'

The Professor signalled another round. 'Does that affect the village?'

'Course it does. We rent our cottages from old Mr Finch, but the young 'un, he doesn't want to know. The new owner, when they get one, will probably put up the rents or turn us out.'

'But you could talk to young Mr Finch…'

'Him? Smooth, he is. Always smiling and wouldn't lift a finger to save his granny.'

Driving back home later, the Professor reflected that, even allowing for exaggeration, Gregory Finch was the last man in the world he would allow Philly to marry…

He had a busy week ahead of him, so there

was no chance to go and see Philly before the following weekend. Sybil was clever enough not to demand to be taken out, being charmingly sympathetic over his long days at the hospital and only once mentioning Gregory.

'He seems so happy,' she told James. 'He sees Philly most days—he's moved into the local pub so's to be nearer to her.' She gave a little laugh. 'He can't talk of anyone else.'

None of which was true. But how was the Professor to know that?

His busy week ended in an even busier weekend, so it wasn't until Monday morning that he got into the Bentley and drove to Nether Ditchling.

The Vicarage door, as usual, was half-open, and somewhere beyond it someone was Hoovering.

Mrs Selby came to the door when he rang. 'Oh, how nice to see you again. Come on in. Did you want to see the Vicar? He's in his study.'

'I wanted to see Philly.'

Mrs Selby shot him a quick look. 'She's in the garden, right at the end, hanging out the washing. Go and find her and I'll put the coffee on.'

Philly, in a cotton dress which was a bit faded, her hair tied back with a piece of string, was pegging sheets with the expertise of long practice.

The Professor didn't speak until he was close behind her, and then his, 'Good morning Philly,' was uttered very quietly.

Philly turned sharply round. 'Whatever are you doing here on a Monday morning? Shouldn't you be working?'

Which was hardly a good start to a conversation.

He said meekly, 'Sometimes I have a day off.'

He took a flapping sheet from her and pegged it neatly. 'I want to talk to you, Philly.'

She shook out a towel. 'Is Sybil with you?'

'No, this is something which concerns us.'

He took the towel from her and hung it up neatly.

Philly picked up a sheet and had it taken from her too.

'Will you listen, Philly?'

'No.' Then, much too brightly, she said, 'Gregory tells me that you and Sybil are to marry very soon. I hope you will both be very happy.'

'You believed him?'

'Of course.' She hadn't wanted to, but he had sounded so convincing. She had cried her eyes out that night, and then in the cold light of morning had resolved never to think of the Professor again.

The Professor sighed. 'Are you going to marry this Gregory?'

'I shan't tell you,' said Philly, turning her back smartly and hanging another sheet. 'And now, go away, do!'

He went, for there was no point in talking to her until she would listen.

At the house Mrs Selby met him as he went through the kitchen door.

'Coffee?' she offered, and then, seeing his face, added, 'Perhaps you would rather not stop?'

He smiled. 'I'll come again, if I may. Tell me, Mrs Selby, does Philly mean to marry Gregory Finch?'

'Marry him! Great goodness, no. She

doesn't like him overmuch, and he certainly doesn't mean to marry her—although he's always on the doorstep. It's as though he's…' she paused to think '…acting a part.'

The Professor nodded; Philly had sent him away, but there was a reason for that and it certainly wasn't because she intended to marry Gregory. If it was because she thought that he and Sybil were to marry, then that was a misunderstanding he must put right.

He should have felt disappointed by her reception of him, but, driving back to London, he felt elated. Sybil and Gregory were somehow concerned in fabricating the man's assiduous courting of Philly; he must see them both as soon as possible.

He went straight to the hospital. Philly might be the love of his life, but his work was his life too.

It was several days before he had the good fortune to meet Sybil and Gregory together.

He had lunched with a colleague, and with an hour or so to spare was walking back to the hospital. Outside an elegant little café he saw

Sybil and Gregory, their heads together over a small table.

Interesting, reflected the Professor; Sybil had phoned to say that she would be staying with friends in Wales for several days. She had also told him that Gregory was still in Nether Ditchling. 'I hear wedding bells,' she had said laughingly.

The Professor strolled across the pavement and took a chair between them. 'Am I interrupting something?' he asked pleasantly. 'Are you hatching another instalment of Gregory's love-life?' He turned a cold eye on him. 'If you so much as set foot in Nether Ditchling again I'll break every bone in your body. Now, tell me why you have been acting the eager bridegroom.'

Gregory had gone pale. He wasn't a brave man, and the Professor's nasty smile and the very size of him sent his heart into his boots.

'It was just a joke. I meant no harm. I did it to please Sybil.'

He ignored the curl of the Professor's lip and Sybil's quick, 'Shut up, Gregory.'

'She was afraid you'd gone off her; after all, no girl likes to see a comfortable future go down the drain. Only she wanted a bit of fun first. It was a good scheme; I'd put you off Philly and you'd forget her…' His voice trailed away. 'Well,' he mumbled, 'there's no harm done…'

'Don't believe a word of it,' said Sybil. 'I may have mentioned that it would be rather a joke to get Philly interested, but that's all.'

The Professor got up, towering over them. 'What a despicable pair you are. If I ever meet you again, Finch, I'll not answer for my actions. And as for you, Sybil, there is a great deal that I would like to say, but what would be the point? I'm sure you will find yourself a husband without difficulty. I'll see that a notice goes into the right papers with the usual polite nonsense used for broken engagements.'

'You wouldn't,' gasped Sybil. 'I'll marry you when you want…'

'But I don't want.' He smiled coldly at them in turn, and then walked away.

* * *

It was almost another week before the Professor was free to drive to Nether Ditchling. It was early afternoon by the time he got there.

The Vicar was putting the finishing touches to his Sunday sermon and Mrs Selby was on the drawing-room sofa with her feet up. All five of her daughters were home, but they were all out, and an hour with a good book was something she had been looking forward to.

She frowned when she heard someone at the open front door and got unwillingly to her feet. But the frown disappeared when she saw the Professor standing there.

'I've disturbed you.' She was still clutching her book. 'I'm so sorry. I've come to see Philly.'

Mrs Selby beamed. 'She's in the church, doing the flowers.' She glanced at the hall clock. 'She must be almost finished.'

He nodded, smiled slowly at her, went back to the street and across to the church. She watched him going inside before going back to the sofa. Not to read this time but to make plans—the plans a bride's mother had such pleasure in making.

Philly was arranging a vase of flowers in one of the side chapels: lupins and phlox, sweet-smelling syringa and floribunda roses. James sat down quietly in a nearby pew and watched her.

When she had finished to her satisfaction he said quietly, 'Philly, will you leave your flowers for a minute and come with me?'

She turned to look at him, her face suddenly aglow with happiness, and went to him and put her hand in his. Together they went out of the church, across the quiet churchyard and into the narrow lane beyond.

'We will talk later,' said the Professor, and took her in his arms and kissed her in a masterful fashion.

Really, there was no need to say anything, reflected Philly, completely and utterly happy. When she was being kissed in such a way words were unnecessary. She looked up into his face and saw the love there. She smiled at him, and then stretched up to kiss him, too.

THE PROPOSAL

CHAPTER ONE

THE HAZY early morning sun of September had very little warmth as yet, but it turned the trees and shrubs of the park to a tawny gold, encouraging the birds to sing too, so that even in the heart of London there was an illusion of the countryside.

The Green Park was almost empty so early in the day; indeed the only person visible was a girl, walking a Yorkshire terrier on a long lead. She was a tall girl with a tawny mane of hair and vivid blue eyes set in a pretty face, rather shabbily dressed; although her clothes were well cut they were not in the height of fashion.

She glanced at her watch; she had walked rather further than usual so Lady Mortimor, although she wouldn't be out of bed herself, would be sure to enquire of her maid if the early morning walk with Bobo had taken the exact time allowed for it. She could have walked for hours… She was on the point of turning on her heel when something large, heavy and furry cannoned into her from the back and she sat down suddenly and in a most unladylike fashion in a tangle of large dog, a hysterical Bobo and Bobo's lead. The dog put an enormous paw on her chest and grinned happily down at her before licking her cheek gently and then turning his attention to Bobo; possibly out of friendliness he kept his paw on her chest, which made getting to her feet a bit of a problem.

A problem solved by the arrival of the dog's owner—it had to be its owner, she decided… only a giant could control a beast of such size and this man, from her horizontal position, justified the thought; he was indeed large, dressed in trousers and a pullover and, even from upside-down, handsome. What was more, he was smiling…

He heaved her to her feet with one hand and began to dust her down. 'I do apologise,' he told her in a deep, rather slow voice. 'Brontes has a liking for very small dogs…'

The voice had been grave, but the smile tugging at the corners of his thin mouth annoyed her. 'If you aren't able to control your dog you should keep him on a lead,' she told him tartly, and then in sudden fright, 'Where's Bobo? If he's lost, I'll never—'

'Keep calm,' begged the man in a soothing voice which set her teeth on edge, and whistled. His dog bounded out from the bushes near by and his master said, 'Fetch,' without raising his voice and the animal bounded off again to reappear again very shortly with Bobo's lead between his teeth and Bobo trotting obediently at the other end of it.

'Good dog,' said the man quietly. 'Well, we must be on our way. You are quite sure you are not hurt?' He added kindly, 'It is often hard to tell when one is angry as well.'

'I am not angry, nor am I hurt. It was lucky for you that I wasn't an elderly dowager with a Peke.'

'Extremely lucky. Miss…?' He smiled

again, studying her still cross face from under heavy lids. 'Renier Pitt-Colwyn.' He offered a hand and engulfed hers in a firm grasp.

'Francesca Haley. I—I have to go.' Curiosity got the better of good sense. 'Your dog—that's a strange name?'

'He has one eye….'

'Oh, one of the Cyclopes. Goodbye.'

'Goodbye, Miss Haley.' He stood watching her walking away towards the Piccadilly entrance to the park. She didn't look back, and presently she broke into an easy run and, when Bobo's little legs could no longer keep up, scooped him into her arms and ran harder as far as the gate. Here she put him down and walked briskly across the road into Berkeley Street, turned into one of the elegant, narrow side-streets and went down the area steps of one of the fine houses. One of Lady Mortimor's strict rules was that she and Bobo should use the tradesmen's entrance when going for their thrice-daily outings. The magnificent entrance hall was not to be sullied by dirty paws, or for that matter Francesca's dirty shoes.

The door opened onto a dark passage with white-washed walls and a worn lino on the floor; it smelled of damp, raincoats, dog and a trace of cooked food, and after the freshness of the early morning air in the park it caused Francesca's nose to wrinkle. She opened one of the doors in the passage, hung up the lead, dried Bobo's paws and went through to the kitchen.

Lady Mortimor's breakfast tray was being prepared and her maid, Ethel, was standing by the table, squeezing orange juice. She was an angular woman with eyes set too close together in a mean face, and she glanced at the clock as Francesca went in, Bobo under one arm. Francesca, with a few minutes to spare, wished her good morning, adding cheerfully, 'Let Lady Mortimor know that Bobo has had a good run, will you, Ethel? I'm going over for my breakfast; I'll be back as usual.' She put the little dog down and the woman nodded surlily. Bobo always went to his mistress's room with her breakfast tray and that meant that Francesca had almost an hour to herself before she would begin her duties as secretary-companion to that lady. A title which hardly fitted the manifold odd jobs which filled her day.

She went back out of the side-door and round to the back of the house, past the elegant little garden to the gate which led to the mews behind the terrace of houses. Over the garage she had her rooms, rather grandly called by Lady Mortimor a flat, where she and her young sister lived. The flat was the reason for her taking the job in the first place, and she was intent on keeping it, for it made a home for the pair of them and, although Lady Mortimor made it an excuse for paying her a very small salary, at least they had a roof over their heads.

Lucy was up and dressed and getting their breakfast. She was very like her sister, although her hair was carroty instead of tawny and her nose turned up. Later on, in a few years' time, she would be as pretty as Francesca, although at fourteen she anguished over her appearance, her ambition being to grow up as quickly as possible, marry a very rich man and live in great comfort with

Francesca sharing her home. An arrangement, Francesca had pointed out, which might not suit her husband. 'I hate you working for that horrid old woman,' Lucy had said fiercely.

'Well, love,' Francesca had been matter-of-fact about it, 'it's a job and we have a home of sorts and you're being educated. Only a few more years and you will have finished school and embarked on a career which will astonish the world and I shall retire.'

Now she took off her cardigan and set about laying the table in the small sitting-room with its minute alcove which housed the cooking stove and the sink.

'I had an adventure,' she said to her sister, and over the boiled eggs told her about it.

'What kind of a dog?' Lucy wanted to know.

'Well, hard to tell—he looked like a very large St Bernard from the front, but he sort of tapered off towards the tail, and that was long enough for two dogs. He was very obedient.'

'Was the man nice to him?' asked Lucy anxiously, having a soft spot for animals; indeed, at that very moment there was a stray mother cat and kittens living clandestinely in a big box under the table.

'Yes—he didn't shout and the dog looked happy. It had one eye—I didn't have time to ask why. It had a funny name, too—Brontes—that's—'

'I know—one of the Cyclopes. Could you meet the man again and ask?'

Francesca thought about it. 'Well, no, not really…'

'Was he a nice man?'

'I suppose so.' She frowned. 'He thought it was funny, me falling over.'

'I expect it was,' said Lucy. 'I'd better go or I'll miss the bus.'

After Lucy had gone she cleared away the breakfast things, tidied the room and their bedroom, and made sure that she herself was tidy too, and then she went back to the house. She was expected to lunch off a tray at midday and she seldom got back until six o'clock each evening; she arranged food for the cat, made sure that the kittens were alive and well, and locked the door.

Her employer was still in bed, sitting up against lacy pillows, reading her letters. In her youth Lady Mortimor had been a handsome woman; now in her fifties, she spent a good part of her days struggling to retain her looks. A face-lift had helped; so had the expert services of one of the best hairdressers in London and the daily massage sessions and the strict diet, but they couldn't erase the lines of discontent and petulance.

Francesca said good morning and stood listening to the woman's high-pitched voice complaining of lack of sleep, the incompetence of servants and the tiresome bills which had come in the post. When she had finished Francesca said, as she nearly always did, 'Shall I attend to the bills first, Lady Mortimor, and write the cheques and leave them for you to sign? Are there any invitations you wish me to reply to?'

Lady Mortimor tossed the pile of letters at her. 'Oh, take the lot and endeavour to deal with them—is there anything that I should know about this morning?'

'The household wages,' began Francesca, and flushed at Lady Mortimor's snide,

'Oh, to be sure you won't forget those…'

'Dr Kennedy is coming to see you at eleven o'clock. Will you see him in the morning-room?'

'Yes, I suppose so; he really must do something about my palpitations—what else?'

'A fitting for two evening gowns at Estelle, lunch with Mrs Felliton.'

'While I am lunching you can get my social diary up to date, do the flowers for the dining-room, and go along to the dry-cleaners for my suit. There will be some letters to type before you go, so don't idle away your time. Now send Ethel to me, have the cheques and wages book ready for me by half-past ten in the morning-room.' As Francesca went to the door she added, 'And don't forget little Bobo…'

'Thank you or please would be nice to hear from time to time,' muttered Francesca as she went to get the wages book, a weekly task which at least gave her the satisfaction of paying herself as well as the rest of the staff.

She entered the amounts, got out the cash box from the wall safe and put it ready for Lady Mortimor, who liked to play Lady Bountiful on Fridays and pay everyone in cash. The bills took longer; she hadn't quite finished them when Maisie, the housemaid, brought her a cup of coffee. She got on well with the staff— with the exception of Ethel, of course; once they saw that she had no intention of encroaching on their ground, and was a lady to boot, with a quiet voice and manner, they accepted her for what she was.

Lady Mortimor came presently, signed the cheques, handed out the wages with the graciousness of royalty bestowing a favour and, fortified with a tray of coffee, received Dr Kennedy, which left Francesca free to tidy the muddled desk she had left behind her and take Bobo for his midday walk, a brisk twenty minutes or so before she went back to eat her lunch off a tray in the now deserted morning-room. Since the lady of the house was absent, Cook sent up what Maisie described as a nice little bit of hake with parsley sauce, and a good, wholesome baked custard to follow.

Francesca ate the lot, drank the strong tea which went with it and got ready to go to the cleaners. It wasn't far; Lady Mortimor patronised a small shop in Old Bond Street and the walk was a pleasant one. The day had turned out fine as the early morning had indicated it might and she allowed her thoughts to roam, remembering wistfully the pleasant house in Hampstead Village where they had lived when her parents had been alive. That had been four years ago now; she winced at the memory of discovering that the house had been mortgaged and the debts so large that they had swallowed up almost all the money there was. The only consolation had been the trust set aside for Lucy's education so that she had been able to stay on as a day pupil at the same well-known school.

There had been other jobs of course, after learning typing and shorthand at night-school while they lived precariously with her mother's elderly housekeeper, but she had known that she would have to find a home of their own as quickly as possible. Two years ago she had answered Lady Mortimor's advertisement and since it offered a roof over their heads and there was no objection to Lucy, provided she never entered the house, she had accepted it, aware that her wages were rather less than Maisie's and knowing that she could never ask for a rise: Lady Mortimor would point out her free rooms and all the advantages of working in a well-run household and the pleasant work.

All of which sounded all right but in practice added up to ten hours a day of taking orders with Sundays free. Well, she was going to stay until Lucy had finished school—another four years. I'll be almost thirty, thought Francesca gloomily, hurrying back with the suit; there were still the flowers to arrange and the diary to bring up to date, not to mention the letters and a last walk for Bobo.

It was pouring with rain the next morning, but that didn't stop Bobo, in a scarlet plastic coat, and Francesca, in a well-worn

Burberry, now in its tenth year, going for their morning walk. With a scarf tied over her head, she left Lucy getting dressed, and led the reluctant little dog across Piccadilly and into the Green Park. Being Saturday morning, there were very few people about, only milkmen and postmen and some over-enthusiastic joggers. She always went the same way for if by any evil chance Bobo should run away and get lost, he had more chance of staying around a part of the park with which he was familiar. The park was even emptier than the streets and, even if Francesca had allowed herself to hope that she might meet the man and his great dog, common sense told her that no one in their right mind would do more than give a dog a quick walk through neighbouring streets.

They were halfway across the park, on the point of turning back, when she heard the beast's joyful barking and a moment later he came bounding up. She had prudently planted her feet firmly this time but he stopped beside her, wagging his long tail and gently nuzzling

Bobo before butting her sleeve with his wet head, his one eye gleaming with friendliness.

His master's good-morning was genial. 'Oh, hello,' said Francesca. 'I didn't expect you to be here—the weather's so awful.'

A remark she instantly wished unsaid; it sounded as though she had hoped to meet him. She went pink and looked away from him and didn't see his smile.

'Ah—but we are devoted dog owners, are we not?' he asked easily. 'And this is a good place for them to run freely.'

'I don't own Bobo,' said Francesca, at pains not to mislead him. 'He belongs to Lady Mortimor; I'm her companion.'

He said, half laughing, 'You don't look in the least like a companion; are they not ladies who find library books and knitting and read aloud? Surely a dying race.'

If he only knew, she thought, but all she said cheerfully was, 'Oh, it's not as bad as all that, and I like walking here with Bobo. I must go.'

She smiled at him from her pretty, sopping-wet face. 'Goodbye, Mr Pitt-Colwyn.'

'*Tot ziens,* Miss Francesca Haley.'

She bent to pat Brontes. 'I wonder why he has only one eye?' she said to herself more than to him, and then walked briskly away, with Bobo walking backwards in an effort to return to his friend. Hurrying now, because she would be late back, she wondered what he had said instead of goodbye—something foreign and, now she came to think of it, he had a funny name too; it had sounded like Rainer, but she wasn't sure any more.

It took her quite a while to dry Bobo when they got back, and Ethel, on the point of carrying Lady Mortimor's tray upstairs, looked at the kitchen clock in triumph.

Francesca saw the look. 'Tell Lady Mortimor that I'm late back, by all means,' she said in a cool voice. 'You can tell her too that we stayed out for exactly the right time but, unless she wishes Bobo to spoil everything in her bedroom, he needs to be thoroughly dried. It is raining hard.'

Ethel sent her a look of dislike and Cook, watching from her stove, said comfortably,

'There's a nice hot cup of tea for you, Miss Haley; you drink it up before you go to your breakfast. I'm sure none of us wants to go out in such weather.'

Ethel flounced away, Bobo at her heels, and Francesca drank her tea while Cook repeated all the more lurid news from the more sensational Press. 'Don't you take any notice of that Ethel, likes upsetting people, she does.'

Francesca finished her tea. 'Well, she doesn't need to think she'll bother me, Cook, and thanks for the tea, it was lovely.'

Lucy would be home at midday since it was Saturday, and they made the shopping list together since she was the one who had to do it.

'Did you see him again?' asked Lucy.

'Who?' Francesca was counting out the housekeeping money. 'The man and his great dog? Yes, but just to say good morning.' She glanced up at her sister. 'Do you suppose I should go another way round the park? I mean, it might look as though I was wanting to meet him.'

'Well don't you?'

'He laughs at me—oh, not out loud, but behind his face.'

'I shall come with you tomorrow and see him for myself.'

On Sundays Francesca took Bobo for his morning run before being allowed the rest of the day free. 'He's not likely to be there so early on a Sunday...'

'All the same, I'll come. What shall we do tomorrow? Could we go to Regent Street and look at the shops? And have something at McDonald's?'

'All right, love. You need a winter coat...'

'So do you. Perhaps we'll find a diamond ring or a string of pearls and get a reward.'

Francesca laughed. 'The moon could turn to cheese. My coat is good for another winter— I've stopped growing but you haven't. We'll have a good look around and when I've saved enough we'll buy you a coat.'

Lady Mortimor had friends to lunch which meant that Francesca had to do the flowers again and then hover discreetly in case her employer needed anything.

'You may pour the drinks,' said Lady Mortimor graciously, when the guests had settled themselves in the drawing-room, and then in a sharp aside, 'And make sure that everyone gets what she wants.'

So Francesca went to and fro with sherry and gin and tonic and, for two of the ladies, whisky. Cool and polite, aware of being watched by critical eyes, and disliking Lady Mortimor very much for making her do something which Crow the butler should be doing. Her employer had insisted that when she had guests for lunch it should be Francesca who saw to the drinks; it was one of the spiteful gestures she made from time to time in order, Francesca guessed, to keep her in her place. Fortunately Crow was nice about it; he had a poor opinion of his mistress, the widow of a wholesale textile manufacturer who had given away enough money to be knighted, and he knew a lady born and bred when he saw Francesca, as he informed Cook.

When the guests had gone, Lady Mortimor went out herself. 'Be sure and have those letters ready for me—I shall be back in time to dress,' she told Francesca. 'And be sure and make a note in the diary—Dr Kennedy is bringing a specialist to see me on Tuesday morning at ten o'clock. You will stay with me of course—I shall probably feel poorly.'

Francesca thought that would be very likely. Eating too much rich food and drinking a little too much as well... She hoped the specialist would prescribe a strict diet, although on second thoughts that might not do—Lady Mortimor's uncertain temper might become even more uncertain.

Sundays were wonderful days; once Bobo had been taken for his walk she was free, and even the walk was fun for Lucy went with her and they could talk. The little dog handed over to a grumpy Ethel, they had their breakfast and went out, to spend the rest of the morning and a good deal of the afternoon looking at the shops, choosing what they would buy if they had the money, eating sparingly at McDonald's and walking back in the late afternoon to tea in the little sitting-room and an evening by the gas fire with the cat and kittens in their box between them.

Monday always came too soon and this time there was no Brontes to be seen, although the morning was fine. Francesca went back to the house to find Lady Mortimor in a bad temper so that by the end of the day she wanted above all things to rush out of the house and never go back again. Her ears rang with her employer's orders for the next day. She was to be earlier than usual—if Lady Mortimor was to be ready to be seen by the specialist then she would need to get up earlier than usual, which meant that the entire household would have to get up earlier too. Francesca, getting sleepily from her bed, wished the man to Jericho.

Lady Mortimor set the scene with all the expertise of a stage manager; she had been dressed in a velvet housecoat over gossamer undies, Ethel had arranged her hair in artless curls and tied a ribbon in them, and she had made up carefully with a pale foundation. She had decided against being examined in her bedroom; the *chaise-longue* in the dressing-room adjoining would be both appropriate and convenient. By half-past nine she was lying, swathed in shawls, in an attitude of resigned long-suffering.

There was no question of morning coffee, of course, and that meant that Francesca didn't get any either. She was kept busy fetching the aids Lady Mortimor considered vital to an invalid's comfort: eau-de-Cologne, smelling salts, a glass of water…

'Mind you pay attention,' said that lady. 'I shall need assistance from time to time and probably the specialist will require things held or fetched.'

Francesca occupied herself wondering what these things might be. Lady Mortimor kept talking about a specialist, but a specialist in what? She ventured to ask and had her head bitten off with, 'A heart consultant of course, who else? The best there is—I've never been one to grudge the best in illness…'

Francesca remembered Maisie and her scalded hand a few months previously. Lady Mortimor had dismissed the affair with a wave of the hand and told her to go to Out-patients during the hour she had off each afternoon. Her tongue, itching to give voice to her strong feelings, had to be held firmly between her teeth.

Ten o'clock came, with no sign of Dr Kennedy and his renowned colleague, and Lady Mortimor, rearranging herself once again, gave vent to a vexed tirade. 'And you, you stupid girl, might have had the sense to check with the consulting-rooms to make sure that this man has the time right. Really, you are completely useless...'

Francesca didn't say a word; she had lost her breath for the moment, for the door had opened and Dr Kennedy followed by Mr Pitt-Colwyn were standing there. They would have heard Lady Mortimor, she thought miserably, and would have labelled her as a useless female at everyone's beck and call.

'Well, can't you say something?' asked Lady Mortimor and at the same time became aware of the two men coming towards her, so that her cross face became all charm and smiles and her sharp voice softened to a gentle, 'Dr Kennedy, how good of you to come. Francesca, my dear, do go and see if Crow is bringing the coffee—'

'No coffee, thank you,' said Dr Kennedy. 'Here is Professor Pitt-Colwyn, Lady Mortimor. You insisted on the best heart specialist, and I have brought him to see you.'

Lady Mortimor put out a languid hand. 'Professor—how very kind of you to spare the time to see me. I'm sure you must be a very busy man.'

He hadn't looked at Francesca; now he said with grave courtesy, 'Yes, I am a busy man, Lady Mortimor.' He pulled up a chair and sat down. 'If you will tell me what is the trouble?'

'Oh, dear, it is so hard to begin—I have suffered poor health every day since my dear husband died. It is hard to be left alone at my age—with so much life ahead of me.' She waved a weak hand. 'I suffer from palpitations, Professor, really alarmingly so; I am convinced that I have a weak heart. Dr Kennedy assures me that I am mistaken, but you know what family doctors are, only too anxious to reassure one if one is suffering from some serious condition…'

Professor Pitt-Colwyn hadn't spoken, there was no expression upon his handsome face and Francesca, watching from her discreet corner, thought that he had no intention of speaking, not at the moment at any rate. He allowed his patient to ramble on in a faint voice, still saying nothing when she paused to say in a quite different tone, 'Get me some water, Francesca, can't you see that I am feeling faint? And hurry up, girl.'

The glass of water was within inches of her hand. Francesca handed it, quelling a powerful desire to pour its contents all over Lady Mortimor's massive bosom.

She went back to her corner from where she admired the professor's beautiful tailored dark grey suit. He had a nice head too, excellent hair—she considered the sprinkling of grey in it was distinguished—and he had nice hands. She became lost in her thoughts until her employer's voice, raised in barely suppressed temper, brought her back to her surroundings.

'My smelling salts—I pay you to look after me, not stand there daydreaming—' She remembered suddenly that she had an audience and added in a quite different voice, 'Do forgive me—I become so upset when I have one of these turns, I hardly know what I'm saying.'

Neither man answered. Francesca administered the smelling salts and the professor got to his feet. 'I will take a look at your chest, Lady Mortimor,' and he stood aside while Francesca removed the shawls and the housecoat and laid a small rug discreetly over the patient's person.

The professor had drawn up a chair, adjusted his stethoscope and begun his examination. He was very thorough and when he had done what was necessary he took her blood-pressure, sat with Lady Mortimor's hand in his, his fingers on her pulse.

Finally he asked, 'What is your weight?'

Lady Mortimor's pale make-up turned pink. 'Well, really I'm not sure...' She looked at

Francesca, who said nothing, although she could have pointed out that within the last few months a great many garments had been let out at the seams...

'You are overweight,' said the professor in measured tones, 'and that is the sole cause of your palpitations. You should lose at least two stone within the next six months, take plenty of exercise—regular walking is to be recommended—and small light meals and only moderate drinking. You will feel and look a different woman within that time, Lady Mortimor.'

'But my heart—'

'It is as sound as a bell; I can assure you that there is nothing wrong with you other than being overweight.'

He got up and shook her hand. 'If I may have a word with Dr Kennedy—perhaps this young lady can show us somewhere we can be private.'

'You are hiding something from me,' declared Lady Mortimor. 'I am convinced that you are not telling me the whole truth.'

His eyes were cold. 'I am not in the habit of

lying, Lady Mortimor; I merely wish to discuss your diet with Dr Kennedy.'

Francesca had the door open and he went past her, followed by Dr Kennedy. 'The morning-room,' she told them. 'There won't be anyone there at this time in the morning.'

She led the way and ushered them inside. 'Would you like coffee?'

The professor glanced at his companion and politely declined, with a courteous uninterest which made her wonder if she had dreamed their meetings in the park. There was no reason why he shouldn't have made some acknowledgement of them—not in front of Lady Mortimor, of course. Perhaps now he had seen her here he had no further interest; he was, she gathered, an important man in his own sphere.

She went back to Lady Mortimor and endured that lady's peevish ill humour for the rest of the day. The next day would be even worse, for by then Dr Kennedy would have worked out a diet.

Of course, she told Lucy when at last she was free to go to her rooms.

'I say, what fun—was he pompous?'

'No, not in the least; you couldn't tell what he was thinking.'

'Oh, well, doctors are always poker-faced. He might have said hello.'

Francesca said crossly, 'Why should he? We haven't anything in common.' She added a little sadly, 'Only I thought he was rather nice.'

Lucy hugged her. 'Never mind, Fran, I'll find you a rich millionaire who'll adore you forever and you'll marry him and live happily ever after.'

Francesca laughed. 'Oh, what rubbish. Let's get the washing-up done.'

As she set out with Bobo the next morning, she wished that she could have taken a different route and gone at a different time, but Lady Mortimor, easy-going when it came to her own activities and indifferent as to whether they disrupted her household, prided herself on discipline among her staff; she explained this to her circle of friends as caring for their welfare, but what it actually meant was that they lived by a strict timetable and since, with the exception of Francesca, she paid them well and Cook saw to it that the food in the kitchen was good and plentiful, they abided by it. It was irksome to Francesca and she was aware that Lady Mortimor knew that; she also knew that she and Lucy needed a home and that not many people were prepared to offer one.

So Francesca wasn't surprised to see Brontes bounding to meet her, followed in a leisurely manner by his master. She was prepared for it, of course; as he drew level she wished him a cold good-morning and went on walking, towing Bobo and rather hampered by Brontes bouncing to and fro, intent on being friendly.

Professor Pitt-Colwyn kept pace with her. 'Before you go off in high dudgeon, be good enough to listen to me.' He sounded courteous; he also sounded as though he was in the habit of being listened to if he wished.

'Why?' asked Francesca.

'Don't be silly. You're bristling with indignation because I ignored you yesterday. Understandable, but typical of the female mind. No logic. Supposing I had come into the room exclaiming, "Ah, Miss Francesca Haley, how delightful to meet you again"—and it was delightful, of course—how would your employer have reacted?' He glanced at her thoughtful face. 'Yes, exactly, I have no need to dot the *I*s or cross the *T*s. Now that that slight misunderstanding is cleared up, tell me why you work for such a tiresome woman.'

She stood still the better to look at him. 'It is really none of your business…'

He brushed that aside. 'That is definitely something I will decide for myself.' He smiled down at her. 'I'm a complete stranger to you; you can say anything you like to me and I'll forget it at once if you wish me to—'

'Oh, the Hippocratic oath.'

His rather stern mouth twitched. 'And that too. You're not happy there, are you?'

She shook her head. 'No, and it's very kind of you to—to bother, but there is really nothing to be done about it.'

'No, there isn't if you refuse to tell me what is wrong.' He glanced at his watch. 'How long do you have before you have to report back?'

'Fifteen minutes.'

'A lot can be said in that time. Brontes and I will walk back with you as far as Piccadilly.'

'Oh, will you?'

'Did I not say so?' He turned her round smartly, and whistled to Brontes. 'Now consider me your favourite uncle,' he invited.

CHAPTER TWO

AFTERWARDS Francesca wondered what had possessed her. She had told Professor Pitt-Colwyn everything. She hadn't meant to, but once she got started she had seemed unable to stop. She blushed with shame just remembering it; he must have thought her a complete fool, sorry for herself, moaning on and on about her life. That this was a gross exaggeration had nothing to do with it; she would never be able to look him in the face again. The awful thing was that she would have to unless he had the decency to walk his dog in another part of the park.

She was barely in the park before he joined her.

'A splendid morning,' he said cheerfully. 'I enjoy the autumn, don't you?' He took Bobo's lead from her and unclipped it. 'Let the poor, pampered beast run free. Brontes will look after him; he has a strong paternal instinct.'

It was difficult to be stand-offish with him. 'He's a nice dog, only he's—he's rather a mixture, isn't he?'

'Oh, decidedly so. Heaven knows where he got that tail.'

For something to say, for she was feeling suddenly shy, 'He must have been a delightful puppy.'

'I found him in a small town in Greece. Someone had poked out his eye and beaten him almost to death—he was about eight weeks old.'

'Oh, the poor little beast—how old is he now?'

'Eight months old and still growing. He's a splendid fellow and strangely enough, considering his origin, very obedient.'

'I must get back.' She looked around for Bobo, who was nowhere in sight, but in answer to her companion's whistle Brontes came trotting up with Bobo scampering beside him. The professor fastened his lead and handed it to her. His goodbye was casually kind; never once, she reflected as she walked back to the house, had he uttered a word about her beastly job. She had been a great fool to blurt out all her worries and grumbles to a complete stranger who had no interest in her anyway. She wished most heartily that there was some way in which she could avoid meeting him ever again.

She thought up several schemes during the course of the day, none of which held water, and which caused her to get absent-minded so that Lady Mortimor had the pleasure of finding fault with her, insisting that she re-type several letters because the commas were in the wrong place. It was after seven o'clock by the time Francesca got back to her room over the garage and found Lucy at her homework.

'You've had a beastly day.' Lucy slammed her books shut and got out a cloth and cutlery. 'I put some potatoes in the oven to bake; they'll be ready by now. We can open a tin of beans, too. The kettle's boiling; I'll make a cup of tea.'

'Lovely, darling, I've had a tiresome day. How's school? Did you get an A for your essay?'

'Yes. Did you see him this morning?'

'Yes, just for a moment…'

'Didn't you talk at all?'

'Only about his dog.' Francesca poured them each a cup of tea and then sat down to drink it. 'I wish I'd never told him—'

'Oh, pooh—I dare say he's forgotten already. He must have lots of patients to think about; his head must be full of people's life histories.'

Francesca opened the tin of beans. 'Yes, of course, only I wish I need never see him again.'

To her secret unacknowledged chagrin, it seemed that she was to have her wish. He wasn't there the following morning, nor for the rest of the week; she told herself that it was a great relief and said so to Lucy, who said, 'Rubbish, you know you want to see him again.'

'Well—yes, perhaps. It was nice to have

someone to talk to.' Francesca went on briskly, 'I wonder if it would be a good idea to go to evening classes when they start next month?'

Lucy looked at her in horror. 'Darling, you must be crazy—you mean sit for two hours learning Spanish or how to upholster a chair? I won't let you. Don't you see the kind of people who go to evening classes are very likely like us—without friends and family? Even if you got to know any of them they'd probably moan about being lonely…'

Francesca laughed. 'You know that's not quite true,' she said, 'although I do see what you mean.'

'Good. No evening classes. Doesn't Lady Mortimor have men visitors? She's always giving dinner parties…'

Francesca mentally reviewed her employer's guests; they were all past their prime. Well-to-do, self-satisfied and loud-voiced. They either ignored her in the same way as they ignored Crow or Maisie, or they made vapid remarks like, 'How are you today, little girl?' Which, since she was all of five

feet ten inches tall and splendidly built, was
an extremely silly thing to say.

She said, laughing, 'I can't say I've ever
fancied any of them. I shall wait until you are
old enough and quite grown-up, and when
you've found yourself a millionaire I shall
bask in your reflected glory.' She began to
clear the table. 'Let's get Mum fed while the
kittens are asleep—and that's another
problem…'

September remained fine until the end of the
month, when wind and rain tore away the last
vestiges of summer. Francesca and Bobo
tramped their allotted routine each morning
and returned, Bobo to be fussed over once he
had been dried and brushed, Francesca to
hurry to her rooms, gobble breakfast and dash
back again to start on the hundred and one
jobs Lady Mortimor found for her to do, which
were never done to that lady's satisfaction.
The strict diet to which Professor Pitt-Colwyn
had restricted her might be reducing her
weight, but it had increased her ill humour.
Francesca, supervising the making of a salad-

dressing with lemon juice to accompany the thin slices of chicken which constituted her employer's lunch, wished that he had left well alone. Let the woman be as fat as butter if she wished, she reflected savagely, chopping a head of chicory while she listened to Cook detailing the menu for the dinner party that evening. A pity the professor couldn't hear that; it was dripping with calories…

Because of the dinner party the staff lunch was cold meat and potatoes in their jackets and Francesca, knowing the extra work involved in one of Lady Mortimor's large dinner parties, had hers in the kitchen and gave a hand with the preparations.

All the guests had arrived by the time she left the house that evening; Lady Mortimor, over-poweringly regal in purple velvet, had made her rearrange the flowers in the hall, polish the glasses again, much to Maisie's rage, and then go to the kitchen to make sure that Cook had remembered how to make sweet and sour sauce, which annoyed the talented woman so much that she threatened to curdle it.

'A good thing it's Sunday tomorrow,' said Francesca, eating toasted cheese while Lucy did her homework. 'And I must think of something for the kittens.' They peered at her, snug against their mother in the cardboard box, and the very idea of finding happy homes for them worried her. How was she to know if the homes were happy and what their mother would do without them?

They went to bed presently, and she dreamt of kittens and curdled sauce and Lady Mortimor in her purple, to wake unrefreshed. At least it wasn't raining, and Lucy would go with her and Bobo, and after breakfast they would go and look at the shops, have a snack somewhere and go to evensong at St Paul's.

The house was quiet as she let herself in through the side-entrance, fastened Bobo's lead and led the little dog outside to where Lucy was waiting. There was a nip in the air, but at least it wasn't raining; they set off at a good pace, crossed into the park and took the usual path. They had reached a small clump of trees where the path curved abruptly when

Bobo began to bark, and a moment later Brontes came hurtling round the corner, to leap up to greet Francesca, sniff at Lucy and turn his delighted attention to Bobo, who was yapping his small head off. They had come to a halt, not wishing to be bowled over by the warmth of the big dog's attention, which gave his master ample time to join them.

'Hello—what a pleasant morning.' He sounded as though they had met recently. Francesca knew exactly how long it had been since they had last met—ten days. She bade him good-morning in a chilly voice, and when he looked at Lucy she was forced to add, 'This is my sister, Lucy. Professor Pitt-Colwyn, Lucy.'

Lucy offered a hand. 'I hoped I'd meet you one day,' she told him, 'but of course you've been away. What do you do with your dog? Does he go with you?'

'If it's possible; otherwise he stays at home and gets spoilt. You like him?'

'He's gorgeous. We've got a cat and kittens; I expect Francesca told you that—now the kittens are getting quite big we'll have to find homes for them.' She peeped at her sister's face; she looked cross. 'I'll take Bobo for a run—will Brontes come with me?'

'He'll be delighted. We'll stroll along to meet you.'

'We should be going back,' said Francesca, still very cool.

Lucy was already darting ahead and the professor appeared not to have heard her. 'I wish to talk to you, so don't be a silly girl and put on airs—'

'Well, really—' She stopped and looked up at his bland face. 'I am not putting on airs, and there is nothing for us to talk about.'

'You're very touchy—high time you left that job.' And at her indignant gasp he added, 'Just keep quiet and listen to me.'

He took her arm and began to walk after the fast retreating Lucy and the dogs. 'You would like to leave Lady Mortimor, would you not? I know of a job which might suit you. A close friend of mine died recently, leaving a widow and a small daughter. Eloise was an actress before she married—indeed, she has returned to the stage for short periods since their marriage—now she has the opportunity to go on tour with a play and is desperate to find someone to live in her house, run it for her and look after little Peggy while she is away. The tour is three or four months and then if it is successful they will go to a London theatre. You will have *carte blanche* and the services of a daily help in the house. No days off—but Peggy will be at school so that you should have a certain amount of free time. Peggy goes to a small day school, five minutes' walk from Cornel Mews—'

'That's near Lady Mortimor's—'

'Yes—don't interrupt. Eloise will come home for the very occasional weekend or day, but since the tour is largely in the north of England that isn't likely to be very often. The salary isn't bad...' He mentioned a sum which left Francesca's pretty mouth agape.

'That's—that's...just for a week? Are you sure? Lady Mortimor...I'm not properly trained.'

'You don't need to be.' He looked down his

commanding nose at her. 'Will you consider it?'

'It's not permanent—and what about the cat
and her kittens?'

He said smoothly, 'It will last for several
months, probably longer, and you will find it
easy to find another similar post once you have
a good reference.'

'Lady Mortimor won't give me one.'

'I am an old friend of Eloise; I imagine that
my word will carry sufficient weight. As for
the cat and kittens, they may come and live in
my house; Brontes will love to have them.'

'Oh, but won't your—that is, anyone mind?'

'No. I shall be seeing Eloise later; may I tell
her that you are willing to go and see her?'

'I would have liked time to think about it.'

'Well, you can have ten minutes while I
round up the rest of the party.'

He had gone before she could protest,
walking away from her with long, easy strides.

He had said 'ten minutes' and she suspected
that he had meant what he had said. It sounded
a nice job and the money was far beyond her

wildest expectations, and she wouldn't be at anyone's beck and call.

Prudence told her that she was probably going out of the frying pan into the fire. On the other hand, nothing venture, nothing win. When he came back presently with Lucy chattering happily and a tired Bobo and a still lively Brontes in tow, she said at once, 'All right, I'll go and see this lady if you'll give me her address. Only it will have to be in the evening.'

'Seven o'clock tomorrow evening. Mrs Vincent, two, Cornel Mews. I'll let her know. I shan't be here tomorrow; I'll see you on Tuesday. You're free for the rest of the day?'

For one delighted moment she thought he was going to suggest that they should spend it together, but all he said was, 'Goodbye,' before he started to whistle to Brontes and turned on his heel, walking with the easy air of a man who had done what he had set out to do.

Lucy tucked an arm in hers. 'Now tell me everything—why are you going to see this Mrs Vincent?'

They started to walk back and by the time they had reached the house Lucy knew all about it. They took Bobo into the kitchen and went back to their rooms to make some coffee and talk it over.

'It won't matter whether Mrs Vincent is nice or not if she's not going to be there,' observed Lucy. 'Oh, Fran, won't it be heavenly to have no one there but us—and Peggy of course—I wonder how old she is?'

'I forgot to ask…'

'All that money,' said Lucy dreamily. 'Now we can easily both get winter coats.'

'Well, I must save as much as I can. Supposing I can't find another job?'

'Never cross your bridges until you get to them,' said Lucy. 'Come on, let's go and look at the shops.' She put the kittens back in their box with their mother.

'I'm glad they'll all have a good home,' Francesca said.

'Yes. I wonder where it is?'

'Somewhere suitable for a professor,' said Francesca snappily. It still rankled that he had taken leave of her so abruptly. There was no reason why he shouldn't, of course. He had done his good deed for the day: found help for his friend and enabled her to leave Lady Mortimor's house.

'I shall enjoy giving her my notice,' she told Lucy.

IT SEEMED AS THOUGH Monday would never end but it did, tardily, after a day of Lady Mortimor's deep displeasure vented upon anyone and anything which came within her range, due to an early morning visit to her hairdresser who had put the wrong coloured streaks in her hair. Francesca had been ordered to make another appointment immediately so that this might be remedied at once, but unfortunately the hairdresser had no cancellations. Francesca, relaying this unwelcome news, had the receiver snatched from her and listened to her employer demanding the instant dismissal of the girl who had done her hair that morning, a demand which was naturally enough refused and added to Lady Mortimor's wrath.

'Why not get Ethel to shampoo your hair and re-set it?' Francesca suggested, and was told not to be so stupid, and after that there was no hope of doing anything right... She was tired and a little cross by the time she got to their rooms to find Lucy ready with a pot of tea.

'You drink that up,' she told Francesca bracingly. 'Put on that brown jacket and skirt—I know they're old, but they're elegant—and do do your face.' She glanced at the clock. 'You've twenty minutes.'

It was exactly seven o'clock when she rang the bell of the charming little cottage in Cornel Mews. Its door was a rich dark red and there were bay trees in tubs on either side of it, and its one downstairs window was curtained in ruffled white net. She crossed her fingers for luck and took a deep breath as the door was opened.

The woman standing there was small and slim and as pretty as a picture. Her dark hair was in a fashionable tangle and she wore the kind of make-up it was difficult to separate from natural colouring. She wore a loose shirt over a very narrow short skirt and high-heeled suede boots and she could have been any age between twenty and thirty. She was in fact thirty-five.

'Miss Haley—do come in, Renier has told me all about you...' She ushered Francesca into a narrow hall and opened a door into a surprisingly large living-room. 'Sit down and do have a drink while we get to know each other.'

Francesca sat, took the sherry she was offered and, since for the moment she had had no chance to say a word, she stayed silent.

'Did Renier explain?' asked Mrs Vincent. 'You know what men are, they never listen.'

It was time she said something, thought Francesca. 'He told me that you were going on tour and needed someone to look after your daughter and keep house for you.'

'Bless the darling, he had it right.' Mrs Vincent curled up in a vast armchair with her drink. 'It's just the details—'

'You don't know anything about me,' protested Francesca.

'Oh, but I do, my daily woman is sister to Lady Mortimor's cook; besides, Renier said you were a sensible young woman with a sense of responsibility, and that's good enough for me. When can you come? I'm off at the end of next week.' She didn't give Francesca a chance to speak. 'Is the money all right? All the bills will go to my solicitor, who'll deal with them, and he'll send you a weekly cheque to cover household expenses and your salary. If you need advice or anything he'll deal with it.'

Francesca got a word in at last. 'Your daughter—how old is she? Can she meet me before I come? I have a sister who would have to live here with me.'

'That's fine. She's up in the nursery; I'll get her down.'

Mrs Vincent went out of the room and called up the narrow stairs, and presently a small girl came into the room. She was one of the plainest children Francesca had ever set eyes on: lank, pale hair, a long, thin face, small, dark eyes and an unhappy little mouth.

'She's six years old,' said Mrs Vincent in a detached way. 'Goes to school of course— very bright, so I've been told. Shake hands with Miss Haley, Peggy. She's coming to stay with you while I'm away.'

The child shook hands with Francesca and Francesca kept the small paw in her own for a moment. 'I shall like coming here to live with you,' she said gently. 'I've a sister, too…' She remembered something. 'Have you a cat or a dog to look after?'

The child shook her head. Her mother answered for her. 'My last nanny wouldn't have them in the house, though it's all one to me.' She laughed. 'I'm not here long enough to mind.'

'Then could I bring a kitten with me? Perhaps you would like one of your very own to look after, Peggy?'

The child smiled for the first time; there was an endearing gap in her teeth. 'For my own?' she asked.

'If your mother will allow that.'

'Oh, let the child have a pet if she wants.'

Mrs Vincent added unexpectedly, 'She takes after her father.'

A remark which made everything clear to Francesca; a lovely, fragile creature like Mrs Vincent would find this plain, silent child a handicap now that she was going back on the stage. Probably she loved her dearly, but she wasn't going to let her interfere with her career. She went pink when Mrs Vincent said, 'I've been left comfortably off, but I've no intention of dwindling into a lonely widowhood,' because she might have read her thoughts. She smiled suddenly. 'I shall wait for a decent interval and get married again.'

Francesca watched Peggy's small face; it was stony with misery. She said quickly, 'I'll bring the kitten when I come, shall I? And you can choose a name for it—it's a little boy cat; he's black and white with yellow eyes.'

Peggy slipped a small hand into hers. 'Really? Will he live here with us?'

'Of course, for this will be his home, won't it?'

Eloise poured herself another drink. 'You have no idea what a relief this is—may I call you Francesca? Now when can we expect you?'

'References?' ventured Francesca.

'Renier says you're OK. That's good enough for me; I told you that.'

'I shall have to give a week's notice to Lady Mortimor. I can do that tomorrow.'

'Good. I can expect you in a week's time. Give me a ring and let me know what time of day you'll be coming and I'll make a point of being in. Now have you time to go round the cottage with me?'

It was a small place, but very comfortably furnished with a well-planned kitchen and, on the ground floor, the living-room and, on the floor above, two good-sized bedrooms and a smaller room with a small bathroom leading from it. 'This is the nursery,' said Mrs Vincent. 'Peggy plays here—she's got masses of toys; she's quite happy to amuse herself.'

Francesca wondered about that although she said nothing. 'How long will you be away?' she asked.

'Oh, my dear, how am I to know? The tour

will last three months at least, and with luck will end up at a London theatre; if it doesn't I shall get my agent to find me something else.'

'Yes, of course. Has Peggy any grandparents or cousins who may want to visit?'

'My parents are in America; Jeff's live in Wiltshire, almost Somerset, actually. We don't see much of them.' Something in her voice stopped Francesca from asking any more questions, and presently she bade Mrs Vincent goodbye, and bent to shake Peggy's hand.

'You won't forget the kitten?'

'No, I'll bring him with me, I promise.'

Back in her little sitting-room she told Lucy everything. 'It's a dear little house, you'll love it. I think Peggy is lonely—she's withdrawn—perhaps she misses her father; I don't know how long ago he died. I promised her a kitten—the black and white one. Mrs Vincent didn't mind.'

'You don't like her much, do you?' asked Lucy shrewdly.

'Well, she's charming and friendly and easy-going, but she didn't seem very interested in

Peggy. Perhaps it's hard to stay at home quietly with a small child if you've been used to theatre friends, and perhaps when her husband was alive they went out a lot.'

'It'll be better than Lady Mortimor's, anyway. We had better start packing up tomorrow, and don't forget Professor Pitt-Colwyn is going to take mother cat and the other kittens. Shall you meet him tomorrow?'

'He said he would be there.' She frowned. 'I must be careful what I say about Mrs Vincent; he said he was a close friend of her husband so I expect he is a close friend of hers as well.'

'Do you suppose she's got her eye on him?'

'Don't be vulgar, Lucy. I should think it was very likely, although for all we know he's married already.'

'You'd better ask him—'

'Indeed I will not.'

He was in the park, waiting for her when she got there the next morning with Bobo. It was a bright day with more than a hint of the coming winter's chill and Francesca, an elderly cardigan over her blouse and skirt, wished she had worn something warmer.

He wasted no time on good-mornings but said, 'You're cold; why didn't you wear something sensible? We had better walk briskly.'

He marched her off at a fine pace, with Bobo keeping up with difficulty and Brontes circling around them. 'Well? You saw Eloise Vincent? Are you going to take the job?'

'Yes, I'm going to give Lady Mortimor my notice this morning and let Mrs Vincent know when I'll be going to her.'

'You saw Peggy?'

'Yes.'

He looked down at her thoughtfully. 'And…?'

'She's a quiet little girl, isn't she? I said I would take one of our kittens there for her to look after; her mother said that I might. You will take the mother cat and the other kittens, won't you?'

'Certainly I will. When will it be convenient for me to collect them? One evening? Let me see, I'm free on Thursday after six o'clock. Where exactly do you live?'

'Well, over the garage at the back of the house. There's a side-door; there's no knocker or bell, you just have to thump.'

'Then shall we say between six o'clock and half-past six? Have you a basket?'

'No, I'll get a cardboard box from the kitchen.'

'No need. I'll bring a basket with me. You're quite happy about this job?'

'Yes, thank you. You see, it's much more money and it will be so nice not to be...that is, it will be nice to be on our own.'

'That I can well believe. Are you scared of Lady Mortimor?'

She gave his question careful thought. 'No, not in the least, but she is sometimes rather rude if anything has annoyed her. I have longed to shout back at her but I didn't dare—she would have given me the sack.'

'Well, now you can bawl her out as much as you like, though I don't suppose you will; you've been too well brought up.'

He had spoken lightly, but when she looked at him she saw the mocking little smile. He must think her a spineless creature, dwindling into a dull spinsterhood. He had been kind, but his pity angered her. After all, she hadn't asked him for help. She said in her quiet voice, 'I have to go. Thank you for your help, and we'll have mother cat and the kittens ready for you when you come.' She gave him a stiff smile. 'Goodbye, Professor Pitt-Colwyn.'

She would contrive to be out when he called on Thursday evening, she decided as she made her way back to the house.

She couldn't have chosen a worse time in which to give in her notice. Lady Mortimor had been to a bridge party on the previous day and lost money, something she couldn't bear to do, and over and above that her dressmaker had telephoned to say that the dress she had wanted delivered that morning was not finished. Francesca went into the room in time to hear her employer declaring that it was no concern of hers if the girl working on it was ill, the dress was to be delivered by two o'clock that afternoon. She glanced up when she saw Francesca. 'Better still, I'll send round a girl to collect it and it had better be ready.

'You heard that,' she snapped. 'That stupid woman having the cheek to say I can't have the dress today. I intend to wear it to the Smithers' drinks party this evening. You'll fetch it after lunch.'

She sat down at the little writing-table and glanced through the letters there. 'Bills,' she said peevishly. 'These tradespeople always wanting their money. You'd better see to them, I suppose, Francesca.' She got up. 'I've a hair appointment—see that they're ready for me when I get back.'

Francesca picked up the letters. 'Lady Mortimor, I wish to give you a week's notice as from today.' She laid an envelope on the desk. 'I have put it in writing.'

Lady Mortimor looked as though she had been hit on the head. Her eyes popped from her head, her mouth gaped. When she had her breath she said, 'What nonsense is this? You must be mad, girl. A cushy job and a flat of your own...I won't hear of it.'

'There's nothing you can do about it,' Francesca pointed out reasonably. 'It isn't a cushy job, it's very badly paid, and it surely isn't a flat—it's two small rooms with a minute kitchen and a shower which doesn't work half the time.'

'You'll have difficulty in getting work, I'll see to that. I'll not give you a reference.'

'That won't be necessary. I already have a job to go to and your reference won't be required.'

'Then you can go now, do you hear, you ungrateful girl?'

'Just as you say, Lady Mortimor. You will have to give me two weeks' wages, one in lieu of notice.' She watched her employer's complexion becoming alarmingly red. 'And whom shall I ask to arrange the dinner party for Saturday? And your lunch party on Sunday? Shall I let Ethel have the bills to check? And there will be the invitations for the charity tea party you are giving next week.'

Francesca paused for breath, astonished at herself. Really she had been most unpleasant and deserved to be thrown out of the house for rudeness. She realised that she wouldn't mind that in the least.

Lady Mortimor knew when she was worsted. 'You will remain until the following week.'

'Tuesday evening,' Francesca interpolated gently, ignoring the woman's glare.

'You will send an advertisement to the usual papers this morning. I require letters in the first instance; interviews can be arranged later to suit me.'

'Certainly, Lady Mortimor. Am I to state the salary?'

'No. The flat goes with the job, of course.' She swept to the door. 'It may interest you to know that you have ruined my day. Such ingratitude has cut me to the quick.'

Francesca forbore from saying that, for someone of Lady Mortimor's ample, corseted figure, the cut would have to be really deep.

Naturally a kind girl and seldom critical of other people, she felt guilty once she was alone. She had been most dreadfully rude; she felt thoroughly ashamed of herself. She had almost finished the bills when Maisie came in with her coffee.

'Cor, miss, what a lark—you going away. Mr Crow was just in the hall passing as you might say and 'eard it all. He said as 'ow you gave as good as you got and good luck to you, we all says—treated you something shameful, she 'as, and you a lady and all.'

'Why, Maisie, how very kind of you all. I'm afraid I was very rude…'

'A bit of plain speaking never 'urt no one, miss. I 'opes 'owever that 'oever takes yer place is capable of a bit of talking back.'

Francesca drank her coffee, feeling cheerful again. She wasn't going to apologise, but she would behave as she always had done, however unpleasant Lady Mortimor might choose to be.

She chose to be very unpleasant. It was a good thing that there were no signs of the professor the next morning for she might have burst into tears all over him and wallowed in self-pity, but by Thursday evening she didn't care any more and allowed Lady Mortimor's ill temper and spiteful remarks to flow over her head. Heedful of her decision, she took care not to get to the rooms until well after seven o'clock, only to find the professor sitting in comfort in the only easy-chair in the place, drinking tea from a mug while Brontes brooded in a fatherly fashion over mother cat and the kittens in their box.

'There you are,' said Lucy as Francesca went in. 'We thought you'd never come. There's still tea in the pot. But Renier's eaten all the biscuits; he didn't have time for lunch. Have you had a beastly day?'

'Well, a bit sticky. I say, isn't Brontes sweet?'

The professor had got up from his chair and pushed her gently into it, and had gone to sit on the small wooden chair which creaked under his weight. He said now, 'I shall be away for the next ten days or so; I hope you settle down with Peggy.' His hooded gaze swept over her tired face. 'It's time you had a change, and I think you will find she will be much nicer to live with than your Lady Mortimor.' He got up. 'I must be going.' He scooped the cat and kittens into the basket he had brought with him, while Lucy cuddled the other kitten on her lap. 'I'll take good care of them,' he said. He smiled at them both. *'Tot ziens.'* And when Francesca made an effort to rise he said, 'No, I'll see myself out.'

The room seemed very empty once he had gone.

CHAPTER THREE

THE WEEK SEEMED never-ending, and Lady Mortimor was determined to get the last ounce of work out of Francesca before she left. There had been several answers to the advertisement, but so far the applicants had refused the job. They had turned up their noses at the so-called flat and two of them had exploded with laughter when they had been told their salary. They were, they had pointed out, secretary-companions, not dog minders or errand girls. Lady Mortimor actually had been shaken. 'You will have to remain until someone suitable can take your place,' she had said the day before Francesca was due to leave.

'That won't be possible,' said Francesca. 'I start my new job immediately I leave here.

One of the agencies might have help for you, but only on a daily or weekly basis.'

Lady Mortimor glared at her. 'I am aware of that, but I have no intention of paying the exorbitant fees they ask.' She hesitated. 'I am prepared to overlook your rudeness, Francesca. I am sure that you could arrange to go to this new job, say, in a weeks' time?'

'I am very sorry, Lady Mortimor, but that is impossible.'

She watched her employer sweep out of the room in a towering rage, and went back to making out the last of the cheques for the tradesmen.

The last day was a nightmare she refused to dwell upon. Lady Mortimor gave her not a moment to herself, and when six o'clock came declared that half the things she had told Francesca to do were still not done. Francesca listened quietly, allowing the tirade to flow over her head. 'There is nothing of importance left to do,' she pointed out. 'Whoever can come in place of me can deal with anything I've overlooked. Goodbye, Lady Mortimor.'

She closed the door quietly on her erstwhile employer's angry voice. She had a happier send-off from the staff, and Crow presented her with a potted plant from them all and wished her well. 'For we're all sure you deserve it, miss,' he said solemnly.

She went to join Lucy, and, after a meal, packed the last of their belongings. A taxi would take them the short distance to Cornel Mews in the morning.

Eloise Vincent was waiting for them when they arrived mid-morning. Peggy was at school, she told them. 'My daily woman will fetch her after lunch. I'm up to my eyes packing; I'm off this evening. I've written down all the names and addresses you might need and a phone number in case you should need me urgently, but for heaven's sake don't ring unless it's something dire.' She led the way upstairs. 'You each have a room; I'll leave you to unpack.' She glanced at the cat basket Lucy was holding. 'Is this the kitten? I dare say Peggy will like having him. There's coffee in the kitchen; help yourselves, will you? Lucy's bed is made up. I'm sorry I haven't put clean sheets on the other bed; the room's been turned out, but I had to empty cupboards and drawers—you won't mind doing it?'

She smiled charmingly and went downstairs, leaving them to inspect their new quarters. The rooms were prettily furnished and to have a room of one's own would be bliss. They unpacked and hung everything away and, with the kitten still in his basket, went downstairs. Mrs Wells, the daily cleaner, was in the kitchen. She was a pleasant-faced, middle-aged woman who poured coffee for them, found a saucer of milk for the kitten and offered to do anything to help. 'I've been here quite a while, before poor Dr Vincent died, so I know all there is to know about the place. I come in the mornings—eight o'clock—and go again after lunch,' she offered biscuits, 'though I said I'd fetch Peggy from school before I go home today.'

'Can't we do that?' asked Francesca. 'We have to get to know her, and it's a chance to see where the school is.'

'Well, now, that would be nice. It's at the end of Cornel Road, just round the corner in Sefton Park Street. Mrs Vincent hoped you wouldn't mind having a snack lunch—the fridge is well stocked and you can cook this evening. She is going out to lunch with a friend, but she'll be back by two o'clock and aims to leave around six o'clock—being fetched by car.'

Francesca thought of the questions she wanted answered before Mrs Vincent left. She put down her coffee-cup. 'Perhaps I could talk to her now?'

Eloise Vincent was in the sitting-room, sitting at her desk, a telephone book before her, the receiver in her hand. She looked up and smiled as Francesca went in. 'Settling in?' she asked. 'Mrs Wells is a fount of knowledge if you've any questions.'

'Yes. She's been most helpful. Mrs Vincent, could you spare a moment? Just to tell me what time Peggy goes to bed, if there's anything she won't eat, which friends is she allowed to play with while you are away…?'

'Oh, dear, what a lot of questions. She goes

to bed about seven o'clock, I suppose. She eats her dinner at school and I've been giving her tea about five o'clock. I don't know about her friends. My husband used to take her with him when he went to see his friends; they haven't been here, although on her birthday we had a party, of course—'

'May I have the names of your doctor and dentist?'

Mrs Vincent laughed. 'Oh, get Renier if anything is worrying you. He's Peggy's godfather; he's fond of her. She's never ill, anyway. Now, you really must excuse me— Mrs Wells can tell you anything else you may want to know.'

It was obvious to Francesca that Mrs Vincent had no more time for her. She went back to the kitchen and did a thorough tour of its cupboards and shelves, went through the linen cupboard with Mrs Wells and, when Mrs Vincent had left for her lunch appointment, sat down with Mrs Wells and Lucy to eat sandwiches and drink more coffee.

Peggy came out of school at three o'clock,

and both of them went to fetch her since Mrs Vincent wasn't back. The children came out in twos and threes and Peggy was one of the last, walking slowly and alone.

They went to meet her and she seemed pleased to see them, walking between them, holding their hands, answering their cheerful questions about school politely. Only when Francesca said, 'The kitten's waiting for you,' did she brighten. They spent the rest of the short walk discussing suitable names for him.

Mrs Vincent was back and there was a car before the door, which was being loaded with her luggage by a tall, middle-aged man. He said, 'Hello, Peggy,' without stopping what he was doing.

She said, 'Hello, Mr Seymour,' in a small wooden voice, all her animation gone again.

'You'd better go and say goodbye to your mother,' he told her over his shoulder. 'We're off in a few minutes.'

The three of them went inside and found Mrs Vincent in the sitting-room, making a last-minute phone call. 'Darlings,' she cried in her light, pretty voice, 'I'm going now. Come and say goodbye to your old mother, Peggy, and promise to be a good girl while I'm away. I'll send you lots of postcards and when I can I will telephone to you.' She kissed her small daughter and turned to Francesca. 'I'll be trying to keep in touch,' she said. 'I'm sure you'll do a marvellous job. Let me know how you are getting on from time to time.'

She smiled, looking so pretty and appealing that Francesca smiled back, quelling the uneasy feeling that Eloise Vincent was only too delighted to be starting her theatrical career once more and couldn't wait to get away.

She was prepared for Peggy's tears once her mother had gone, but the child's face had remained impassive. 'May I have the kitten now?' she asked, almost before they were out of sight.

She and the small creature took to each other at once. She sat happily in the sitting-room with him on her small, bony knees, talking to him and stroking his head with a small, gentle hand. 'I shall call him Tom,' she told Francesca.

'That's a nice name.'

'Daddy used to read me a story about Tom Kitten…' The small voice quavered and Francesca said quickly, 'Shall we talk about your daddy? I'd like to know all about him.'

So that was the trouble, she reflected, listening to the child's rambling description of her father and the fun they had had together. Peggy had loved him dearly and there had been no one to talk to her about him. She let the child chat on, the small face animated, and then said gently, 'What nice things you have to remember about him, Peggy, and of course he'll never go away; he'll always be there inside your head.'

'I like you,' said Peggy.

It took a few days to settle into a routine. Lucy went to school each morning and Francesca took Peggy to her school shortly afterwards, going back to make the beds and shop and wash and iron while Mrs Wells gave the house what she called a good tidy up. Tom settled down without any nonsense, aware by now that he belonged to Peggy and no one else, sitting beside her chair at meals and sleeping at the foot of her bed.

There had been no news of Mrs Vincent. Francesca wasn't sure where she was, for the promised list of the various towns the company would be appearing in hadn't turned up. It was a relief that at the end of the week there was a cheque in the post with her salary and a housekeeping allowance.

It was two days later, after they had had tea and Francesca was on the floor in the kitchen, showing Peggy how to play marbles while Tom pranced around them both, that the front doorbell was rung.

'I'll go,' called Lucy, in the sitting-room with her homework, and a moment later Professor Pitt-Colwyn's voice sent Peggy flying to the kitchen door. He caught her in his arms and kissed her soundly. 'Hello, love, I thought it was time I came to see how you were getting on…'

He watched Francesca get up off the floor

and brush down her skirt. 'Marbles—am I in time for a game?' and then he added, 'Good evening, Francesca.'

She was surprised at how glad she was to see him. 'Good evening, Professor.' She scanned his face and saw that he was tired. 'Shall we go into the sitting-room? I'll make a cup of coffee while you and Peggy have a talk—she wants to show you Tom.'

He looked down at the small, earnest face staring up at him. 'A splendid idea—shall we be disturbing Lucy?'

'I've just finished,' said Lucy. 'I'll help Fran get the coffee—'

'A sandwich with it?' asked Francesca.

'That would be very nice.'

'Have you had no lunch or tea?'

'A rather busy day.' He smiled, and she could see that he wasn't going to talk about it.

She made a pot of coffee, cut a plateful of cold beef sandwiches and bore the tray into the sitting-room. Peggy was sitting on the professor's knee and Tom had curled upon her small lap. Francesca was astonished to hear the child's happy voice, talking nineteen to the dozen.

'We are talking about Peggy's father,' said the professor deliberately.

Francesca said at once, 'He must have been a marvellous dad. Peggy has told us a little about him.' She poured him a cup and gave it to him. 'You stay there, darling. Here's your milk, and take care not to spill it over your godfather's trousers.'

She passed the sandwiches too, and watched him eat the lot. 'There's a cake I made this afternoon,' she suggested.

He ate several slices of that too, listening to Peggy's chatter, knowing just when to make some remark to make her giggle. Francesca let her bedtime go by, for the little girl was really happy. It was the professor who said at last, 'It's way past your bedtime, Peggy,' and when she wound her arms round his neck he said, 'If you go to bed like the good girl you are, I'll come and take you to the zoo on Saturday afternoon.'

'Fran and Lucy too?'

'Of course. Tom can mind the house and we'll come back here and have an enormous tea.'

She slid off his knee. Kissed him goodnight then, and went to stand by Francesca's chair. 'Will we?' she asked. 'Will we, really?'

'If your godfather says so, then of course we will, and I'll make a simply enormous cake and we'll have crumpets dripping with butter.'

'Could Lucy put her to bed?' asked the professor. 'We might have a chat?'

'Of course I can.' Lucy scooped up the kitten and handed him to Peggy. 'And Fran will come and tuck you up when you're in bed.'

Peggy went happily enough, her hand in Lucy's and the kitten tucked under one arm. Francesca, suddenly shy, offered more coffee.

'Any problems?' asked the professor.

She thought before she answered. 'No, I don't think so. I should have liked to have known a bit more about Peggy before Mrs Vincent left, but there wasn't much time. Mrs Wells is a great help with things like shopping and so on. Peggy doesn't seem to have any friends…do you suppose it would be all right if I invited one or two children for tea one day? I think she is a very shy little girl.'

'She is a very unhappy little girl. She loved her father very much and she misses him; she likes to talk about him. I think that Eloise didn't understand that and the child is too small to carry so much hidden grief.' He glanced at her. 'She told me that she talks to you and Lucy about him.'

'Yes, he is still alive to her, isn't he? If you're sure that's the right thing to do?'

'Quite sure. By all means see if you can get some children round to play with her. Has she no friends at all at school?'

'Oh, one or two speak to her but she doesn't seem to have any special friends, but I'll do my best. She has masses of toys and it would be nice if she were to share them.'

'Have you heard from Eloise?'

'Me? No. She said she would be too busy rehearsing to write for a while.'

'I'm going to Cheltenham to see the opening

show next week. If you think of anything you want to know about, let me know before then.'

'Thank you. She left everything beautifully organised. I expect she's a very good actress?'

He didn't answer, and she wondered uncomfortably if she had said something about Mrs Vincent which might have annoyed him. She couldn't think of anything but if he was in love with her, and she supposed that he was, he would be touchy about her. Lucy came in then.

'Peggy's bathed and in bed; she 's waiting for you to say goodnight—both of you.'

The child wreathed her arms round Francesca's neck. 'I love you, Fran.'

'Thank you, darling. I love you too, and Tom of course. Now go to sleep quickly, won't you? Because he's asleep already.'

The professor was hugged in his turn, and he was reminded of his promise to take them to the zoo on Saturday, then he was kissed goodnight. 'Now tuck me in, please, Fran.'

So she was tucked in and he stood in the little room, leaning against the wall, watching, his eyes half closed.

Back in the sitting-room he said, 'I must be off. Thanks for the coffee and sandwiches.'

'It made Peggy very happy to see you,' Francesca said. The thought that it had made her very happy too was sternly dismissed. 'You will have a good meal before you go to bed, won't you?'

He looked as though he were going to laugh. 'Indeed I will.' He smiled at Lucy and dropped a large hand on Francesca's shoulder for a moment and went away. Lucy went to the window to watch him drive away, but Francesca busied herself with the cups and saucers.

'I shall enjoy the zoo,' said Lucy.

'Yes, it should be fun; Peggy will love it. Lucy, I must do something about finding her some friends...'

'Well, gossip around when you go to get her from school. I dare say our Eloise discouraged them—children are noisy and they make a mess...'

'You're probably right, but don't call her that, dear—we might forget and say something—I mean, I think he's in love with her, don't you? He's going all the way to Cheltenham for the opening night.'

They were in the kitchen, washing up the coffee-cups.

'That doesn't mean that he's in love with her. What shall we have for supper? It's a bit late.'

The following day Francesca made a few tentative overtures to the mothers and nannies taking the children to school. They were friendly enough, and she made a point of letting them know that Mrs Vincent had gone away for a time and that she was looking after Peggy. She said no more than that, but it was, she thought, the thin end of the wedge...

She wasn't sure, but she thought that maybe the children had been discouraged from getting friendly with Peggy, a child too shy to assert herself with the making of friends. It might take some time, but it would be nice if she could get to know a few children while her mother was away, so that by the time she got back home Peggy would have established a circle of little friends. Already the child was livelier, learning to play the games small children played, spending long hours with Francesca or Lucy rearranging the elaborate doll's house, planning new outfits for the expensive dolls she had. 'Woollies for the winter,' explained Francesca, getting knitting needles and wool and starting on miniature sweaters and cardigans.

They all went shopping the next day, and it was apparent that Peggy had never been to Woolworth's. They spent a long time there while she trotted from one counter to the other, deciding how to spend the pocket money Francesca had given her. After the rigours of Lady Mortimor's household, life was very pleasant. Francesca, going about her chores in the little house, planning meals, playing with Peggy, sitting in the evenings sewing or knitting, with Lucy doing her homework at the table, felt that life was delightful. They had a home, well, not a permanent one, but still a home for the time being—enough money, the prospect of having some new clothes and of adding to their tiny capital at the bank. She was almost content.

The professor came for them after lunch on Saturday, bundled them briskly into his car, and drove to the zoo. It was a mild autumn day, unexpected after several days of chilly rain. Francesca, in her good suit, her burnished hair gleaming in the sunshine, sat beside him in the car making polite small talk, while Lucy and Peggy in the back giggled and chattered together. The professor, who had been up most of the night with a very ill patient, allowed the happy chatter from the back seat to flow over his tired head and listened to Francesca's pretty voice, not hearing a word she said but enjoying the sound of it.

The afternoon was a success; they wandered along, stopping to look at whatever caught their eyes, with Peggy skipping between them until she caught sight of the camels, who were padding along with their burden of small children.

The professor fished some money out of his

pocket and gave it to Lucy. 'You two have a ride; Francesca and I are going to rest our feet. We'll be here when you get back.'

'You make me feel very elderly—bunions and dropped arches and arthritic knees,' protested Francesca, laughing as they sat down on an empty bench.

'You, my dear girl, will never be elderly. That is an attitude of mind.' He spoke lightly, not looking at her. 'You have settled down quite happily, I hope?'

'Oh, yes, and Lucy and Peggy get on famously.'

'So I have noticed. And you, Francesca, you mother them both.'

She was vexed to feel her cheeks grow hot. She asked stiffly, 'How is Brontes? And mother cat and the kittens?'

'He has adopted them. You must come and see them. The children are at school during the day? You will be free for lunch one day? I'll give you a ring.'

'Is that an invitation?' asked Francesca frostily.

'Certainly it is. You want to come, don't you?'

She had no intention of saying so. 'I shall be very glad to see mother cat and the kittens again.'

His stern mouth twitched a little. 'I shall be there too; I hope you will be glad to see me.'

'Well, of course.' She opened her handbag and looked inside and closed it again for something to do. She would be very glad to see him again, only he mustn't be allowed to know that. He was merely being friendly, filling in his days until Eloise Vincent should return. She wished that she knew more about him; she voiced the wish without meaning to and instantly wanted it unsaid.

'You flatter me.' He told her blandly, 'Really there is nothing much to tell. I work—as most men work. Perhaps I am fortunate in liking that work.'

'Do you go to a hospital every day or have a surgery?'

'I go to several hospitals and I have consulting-rooms.'

She persisted. 'If you are a professor, do you teach the students?'

'Yes. To the best of my ability!' He added

gently, 'I examine them too, and from time to time I travel. Mostly to examine students in hospitals in other countries. I have a very competent secretary and a nurse to help me—'

'I'm sorry, I've been very rude; I can't think why I asked you about your work or—or anything.' She had gone pink again and she wouldn't look at him, so that the long, curling lashes, a shade darker than her hair, lay on her cheeks. She looked quite beautiful and he studied her with pleasure, saying nothing. It was a great relief to her when Lucy and Peggy came running towards them. Caught up in the excited chatter from Peggy, she forgot the awkward moment.

They went back to the little house in the Mews presently and had their tea: fairy cakes and a gingerbread, little sandwiches and chocolate biscuits. 'It's like my birthday,' said Peggy, her small, plain face wreathed in smiles.

The professor stayed for an hour after tea, playing ludo on the floor in front of the sitting-room fire. When he got to his feet, towering over them, he observed pleasantly, 'A very nice afternoon—we must do it again some time.' He kissed his small god-daughter, put a friendly arm around Lucy's shoulders, and went to the door with Francesca.

'I'll phone you,' was all he said, 'and thanks for the tea.'

IT WAS several days later when she had a phone call. A rather prim voice enquired if she were Miss Haley and went on to ask if she would lunch with Professor Pitt-Colwyn in two days' time. 'If it wouldn't inconvenience you,' went on the voice, 'would you go to the Regent hospital at noon and ask for the professor?'

Francesca agreed. Were they going to eat at the hospital? she wondered, and what should she wear? It would have to be the brown suit again. Her winter coat was too shabby and although there was some money now Lucy needed a coat far more than she did. She would wash her hair and do her nails, she decided, and buy a new lipstick.

The Regent hospital was in the East End. It

was a hideous building, heavily embellished with fancy brickwork of the Victorian era, brooding over a network of shabby streets. Francesca got off the bus opposite its entrance and presented herself at the reception desk inside the entrance hall.

The clerk appeared to know who she was, for she lifted the phone and spoke into it, and a moment later beckoned to one of the porters.

'If you would wait for a few minutes, Miss Haley, the porter will show you...'

Francesca followed the man, wishing that she hadn't come; she couldn't imagine the professor in this vast, echoing building. Probably he had forgotten that he had invited her and was deep in some highly urgent operation. Come to think of it, she didn't know if he was a surgeon or a physician. She sat down in a small room at the back of the entrance hall, facing a long corridor. It was empty and after a minute or two she was tempted to get up and go home, but all at once there were people in it, walking towards her: the professor, towering above the posse of people trying to keep up with him, a short, stout ward sister, two or three young men in short white coats, an older man in a long white coat, a tall, stern-looking woman with a pile of folders under one arm and, bringing up the rear, a worried-looking nurse carrying more folders.

The professor paused in the doorway of the room she was in, filling it entirely with his bulk. 'Ah, there you are,' he observed in a voice which suggested that she had been in hiding and he had just discovered her. 'Give me five minutes…'

He had gone and everyone else with him, jostling each other to keep up.

He reappeared not ten minutes later, elegant in a dark grey suit and a silk tie which had probably cost as much as her best shoes. They had been her best for some time now, and she hardly ever wore them for they pinched abominably.

'Kind of you to come here,' he told her breezily. 'I wasn't sure of the exact time at which I could be free. Shall we go?'

She walked beside him, out to the space reserved for consultants' cars and got into the car, easing her feet surreptitiously out of her shoes. The professor, watching out of the corner of his eye, turned a chuckle into a cough and remarked upon the weather.

He drove west, weaving his way through the small side-streets until she, quite bewildered by the one-way traffic, saw that they were in Shaftesbury Avenue. But only briefly; he turned into side-streets again and ten minutes or so later turned yet again into a narrow street, its trees bare of leaves now, the houses on either side elegant Regency, each with a very small garden before it, steps leading up to doorways topped by equally elegant fanlights. The professor stopped the car and got out to open her door. 'I thought we might lunch at home,' he told her. 'Brontes is anxious to see you again.'

'You live here?' asked Francesca. A silly question, but she had been surprised; it was, she guessed, five minutes away from Mrs Vincent's cottage.

'Yes.' He took her arm and marched her up the steps as the door was opened by a dignified middle-aged man in a black jacket and pin-striped trousers.

'Ah, Peak. Francesca, this is Peak, who sees that this place runs on oiled wheels. Mrs Peak is my housekeeper. Peak, this is Miss Haley. Show her where she can leave her coat, will you?' He picked up his bag. 'I'll be in the drawing-room, Francesca.'

In the charming little cloakroom concealed beneath the curving staircase, she poked at her hair, added more lipstick and deplored the suit; she had better take off the jacket otherwise it might look as though she were ready to dart out of the house again. Her blouse wasn't new either, but it was ivory silk, laundered and pressed with great care, and the belt around her slender waist was soft leather. Her feet still hurt, but she would be able to ease them out of her shoes again once they were sitting at the table. She went back into the narrow hall and the professor appeared at a half-open door.

'Come and have a drink before lunch.' He held the door wide and Brontes stuck his great head round it, delighted to see her.

The room was long and narrow, with a bay

window overlooking the street and a charming
Adam fireplace. The chairs were large and
deep and well cushioned, and there was a scat-
tering of small lamp tables as well as a
handsome bow-fronted display cabinet embellished with marquetry, its shelves filled
with silver and porcelain. The professor went
to the rent table under the window. He asked,
'Sherry for you? And do sit down.'

She sat, and was aware that mother cat and
her kittens were cosily curled up together in
one of the easy chairs. She said, 'Oh, they
seem very much at home.'

He handed her the sherry. 'Brontes has seen
to that; he is their devoted guardian angel.'

She sipped her sherry, very aware of him
sitting opposite her, Brontes pressed up
against him, both of them watching her. Her
tongue, as it sometimes did, ran away with
her. 'Do you want to tell me something? Is that
why you asked me to lunch?'

'Yes, to both your questions, but it can wait.'
He settled back in his great chair. 'Your sister
is a bright child; has she any ideas about the

future?' It was a casual question and she answered readily enough.

'She's clever; she's set her heart on GCSEs, A levels, and a university.'

'Some discerning young man will snap her up long before then.' He smiled at her. 'And why aren't you married?'

It was unexpected. 'Well, I—I…that is, they weren't the right ones. None of them the right man.'

This muddled statement he received with a gentle smile. 'Have you any messages for Eloise?'

'If you would tell her that Peggy seems happy and is doing well at school and that everything is fine. She hasn't written or phoned, but I expect she's very busy.'

'Undoubtedly,' he agreed gravely. Peak came then to tell them that lunch was ready, and she went with the professor to a smaller room at the back of the house, which overlooked a surprisingly large garden. 'You've got trees, how lovely,' she exclaimed. 'It must look beautiful in the spring.'

They lunched off iced melon, baked salmon in a pastry case and a coffee *bavarois* and, while they ate, the professor kept the conversation quite firmly in his hands; impersonal topics, the kind of talk one might have had with a stranger sharing one's table in a restaurant, thought Francesca peevishly. Back in the drawing-room, drinking coffee from paper-thin cups, she said suddenly, 'I wish you would talk about your work—you looked different at the hospital; it's a side of you that I know nothing about.' She put down her cup. 'I'm sorry, I'm being nosy again.' She looked at her feet, aching in the shoes she longed to kick off. 'Only I'm interested,' she mumbled.

'I have an appointment at half-past two,' he told her. 'I'll drive you back as I go to my rooms, which means that we have half an hour. Do take off those shoes and curl up comfortably.'

'Oh, how did you know? I don't wear them very often and they're a bit tight. You don't mind?'

'Not in the least. What do you want to know about my work, Francesca?'

'Well, I know that you're a professor and a consultant, but are you a surgeon or a physician? You said you went to other hospitals and that you travelled. Why?'

'I'm a surgeon, open-heart surgery valve replacements, by-passes, transplants. Most of my work is at Regent's, but I operate at all the big provincial hospitals if I'm needed. I have a private practice and an out-patients clinic twice a week. I work in Leiden too, occasionally in Germany and the States, and from time to time in the Middle East.'

'Leiden,' said Francesca. 'You said *"tot ziens"* one morning in the park; we looked it up—it's Dutch.'

'My mother is a Dutchwoman; she lives just outside Leiden. I spend a good deal of time there. My father was British; he died two years ago.'

He looked at her, half smiling, one eyebrow raised in a gentle way. The half-smile widened and she thought it was mocking, and went red. He must think her a half-wit with no manners. She plunged into a muddled speech. 'I don't know why I had to be so rude, I do apologise,

I have no excuse, if I were you I wouldn't want to speak to me again—'

He said gently, 'But I'm not you, and fortunately I see no reason why I shouldn't speak to you again. For one thing, it may be necessary from time to time. I did tell Eloise that I would keep an eye on Peggy.'

'Yes, of course. I—I expect that you would like to go now.' She sat up straight and crammed her feet back into her shoes and then stood up. 'Thank you for my lunch—it was delicious.'

He appeared not to notice how awkward she felt. Only as he stopped in Cornel Mews and got out to take the key from her and open the door of the cottage did he say, 'We must have another talk some time, Francesca,' and he bent to kiss her cheek as she went past him into the hall.

CHAPTER FOUR

FRANCESCA WAS sitting by the fire, reading to Peggy, when Lucy came in. 'Well, did you have a good lunch? What did you eat?'

Francesca recited the menu.

'Nice—to think I was chewing on liver and bacon... Where did you go?'

'To his house; it's quite close by.'

Lucy flung down her school books and knelt down by the fire. 'Tell me everything,' she demanded.

When Francesca had finished she said, 'He must be very rich. I expect he's clever too. I wonder what his mum's like.'

'How's school?'

'OK.' Lucy dug into a pocket. 'There's a letter for you, but don't take any notice of it; I don't want to go...'

The words were bravely said but palpably not true. A party of pupils was being organised to go skiing two weeks before Christmas. Two weeks in Switzerland with proper tuition and accompanied by teachers. The fare and the expenses totalled a sum which Francesca had no hope of finding.

'Oh, Lucy, I'm so sorry. If it's any consolation I'll get the money by hook or by crook for next winter.' She glanced at her sister's resolutely cheerful face. 'All your friends are going?'

'Well, most of them, but I really don't mind, Fran. We can have a lovely time here, getting ready for Christmas.'

So nothing more was said about it, although Francesca sat up late, doing sums which, however hard she tried, never added up to enough money to pay for Lucy's skiing holiday. There was enough money set aside for her school fees, of course, but that wasn't to be touched. She went to bed finally with a headache.

There was no postcard from Mrs Vincent; nor was there a phone call. Francesca reminded herself that the professor would be with her, and most likely he would bring back something for Peggy when he returned. The child showed no concern at the absence of news from her mother, although it seemed to Francesca that she was looking pale and seemed listless; even Tom's antics were met with only a half-hearted response. Francesca consulted Mrs Wells. 'I think she should see a doctor. She isn't eating much either. I wonder if she's missing her mother...'

Mrs Wells gave her an old-fashioned look. 'I'm not one for telling tales out of school, but 'er mum never 'as had no time for 'er. Disappointed she was; she so pretty and charming and Peggy as plain as a pikestaff. No, you don't need to fret yerself about that, Miss Haley; little Peggy don't love 'er mum all that much. She was 'appier when her granny and grandpa came to visit. That was when Dr Vincent was alive—loved the child they did, and she loved them.'

So Francesca had done nothing for a few more days, although Peggy didn't seem any better. She had made up her mind to get a doctor by now. If only the professor had phoned, she could have asked his advice, but he, of course, would be wherever Mrs Vincent was. She fetched Peggy from school, gave her her tea which she didn't want and, as soon as Lucy came home, took the child upstairs to bed. Peggy felt hot and she wished she could take her temperature, but there was a singular lack of first-aid equipment in the house, and she blamed herself for not having attended to that. She sat the child on her lap and started to undress her, and as she took off her clothes she saw the rash. The small, thin back was covered with red spots. She finished the undressing, washed the pale little face, and brushed the mousy hair and tucked the child up in bed. 'A nice glass of cold milk,' she suggested, 'and Lucy shall bring it up to you.'

'Tom—I want Tom,' said Peggy in a small voice. 'I've got a pain in my head.'

'You shall have Tom, my dear,' said Francesca and sped downstairs, told Lucy, and went to the phone. Even if the professor were still away, surely that nice man Peak would have a phone number or, failing that, know of a local doctor.

She dialled the number Mrs Vincent had left in her desk and Peak answered.

'Peak, did Professor Pitt-Colwyn leave a phone number? I need to speak to him—Peggy's ill.'

'A moment, Miss Haley,' and a second later the professor's voice, very calm, sounded in her ear.

'Francesca?'

'Oh, so you are there,' she said fiercely. 'Peggy's ill; there's a rash all over her back and she feels sick and listless. She's feverish, but I can't find a thermometer anywhere and I don't know where there's a doctor and I've not heard a word since Mrs Vincent went away—'

'Peggy's in bed? Good. I'll be with you in about ten minutes.' He rang off and she spent a moment with the unhappy thought that she had been anything but calm and sensible; she had even been rather rude...and he had sounded impassive and impersonal, as though she were a patient to be dealt with efficiently. Though I'm not the patient, she thought in a muddled way as she went back to Peggy and sent Lucy downstairs to open the door for the professor, and then sat down on the side of the bed to hold the tearful child in her arms.

She didn't hear him come in; for such a big man he was both quick and silent. She was only aware of him when he put two hands on her shoulders and eased her away from Peggy and took her place.

He was unhurried and perfectly calm and apparently unworried and it was several minutes before he examined the child, took her temperature and then sat back while Francesca made her comfortable again. 'Have you had chicken-pox?' He glanced at Francesca.

'Me? Oh, yes, years ago; so has Lucy.'

'And so have I, and now so has Peggy.' He took the small, limp hand in his. 'You'll feel better very soon, Peggy. Everyone has chicken-pox, you know, but it only lasts a few days. You will take the medicine Francesca will give you and then you'll sleep as soundly as Tom and in the morning I'll come and see you again.'

'I don't want Mummy to come home—'

'Well, love, there really is no need. Francesca will look after you, and as soon as you feel better we'll decide what is to happen next, shall we?' He kissed the hot little head. 'Lucy will come and sit with you until Francesca brings your medicine. *Tot ziens.*'

Peggy managed a watery smile and said, *'Tot ziens.'*

In the sitting-room Francesca asked anxiously, 'She's not ill, is she? I mean, ill enough to let her mother know? She said she didn't want to be—that is, there was no need to ring her unless there was something serious.'

When he didn't answer she added, 'I'm sorry if I was rude on the phone; I was worried and I thought you were away.'

'Now why should you think that?'

'You said you were going to Cheltenham.'

'As indeed I did go.' He was writing a prescription as he spoke. 'Don't worry, Peggy is quite all right. She has a temperature but, having chicken-pox, that is only to be expected. Get this tomorrow morning and see that she takes it three times a day.' He took a bottle from his bag and shook out a tablet. 'This will dissolve in hot milk; it will make her more comfortable and she should sleep.'

He closed his bag and stood up. 'I'll call in on my way to the hospital in the morning, but if you're worried don't hesitate to phone me; I'll come at once.' At the door he turned. 'And don't worry about her mother. I'll be seeing her again in a day or so and then I can reassure her.'

Francesca saw him to the door and wished him a polite goodnight. If it hadn't been imperative that she should see to Peggy at once, she would have gone somewhere quiet and had a good cry. She wasn't sure why she wanted to do this and there really wasn't time to think about it.

Peggy slept all night and Francesca was up and dressed and giving the little girl a drink of lemonade when the professor arrived. He was in flannels and a thick sweater and he hadn't shaved, and she said at once, 'You've been up all night.'

'Not quite all of it. How is Peggy?'

They went to look at her together and he pronounced himself content with her progress. There were more spots now, of course, but her temperature was down a little and she greeted him cheerfully enough. 'Anything in moderation if she's hungry,' he told Francesca, 'and get the elixir started as soon as you can.'

'Thank you for coming. Lucy's made tea—we haven't had our breakfast yet. You'll have a cup?'

He refused pleasantly. 'I must get home and shower and change; I've an out-patients clinic at ten o'clock.'

She opened the door onto a chilly morning.

'I'll look in some time this evening.' He was gone with a casual nod.

It was late in the afternoon when Francesca had a phone call from Peggy's grandmother in Wiltshire. It was a nice, motherly voice with no hint of fussing. 'Renier telephoned. Poor little Peggy, but we are so glad to know that she is being so well looked after. I suppose you haven't heard from her mother?'

'Well, no, the professor said that he would be seeing her and that there was no need to let her know. Peggy is feeling much better and he is looking after her so well, so please don't be anxious.'

'She's our only grandchild and so like our son. He was Renier's friend, you know. They were at university together and school together—he was best man at their wedding and is godfather to Peggy.'

'Would you like to speak to Peggy? She's awake. I'll carry her across to the other bedroom; there's a phone there…'

'That would be delightful. Shall I ring off or wait?'

'If you would wait—I'll be very quick…'

The conversation went on for some time, with Peggy on Francesca's lap, talking non-stop and getting too excited. Presently Francesca whispered, 'Look, Peggy, ask Granny if you can telephone her each day about teatime, and if she says "yes" say goodbye now.'

A satisfactory arrangement for all parties.

The professor came in the evening, once more the epitome of the well-dressed gentleman. He was coolly polite to Francesca, spent ten minutes with Peggy, who was tired and a little peevish now, pronounced himself satisfied and, after only the briefest of conversations, went away again.

'No need to come in the morning,' he observed, 'but I'll take a look about this time tomorrow.'

The next day he told Francesca that Peggy might get up in her dressing-gown and roam the house. 'Keep her warm, she needs a week or so before she goes back to school. You're dealing with the spots, aren't you? She mustn't scratch.'

The next day he told her that he would be seeing Eloise on the following day.

'How nice,' said Francesca tartly. 'I'm sure you will be able to reassure her. Peggy's granny has been phoning each afternoon; she sounds just like a granny...' A silly remark, she realised, but she went on, 'Peggy's very fond of her.'

'Yes, I know. I shall do my best to persuade Eloise to let her go and stay with her for a few days. You will have to go too, of course.'

'But what about Lucy?'

'I imagine that it could be arranged for her to board for a week or so? Eloise will pay, of course. Would Lucy mind?'

'I think she would love it…but it will be quite an expense.'

'Not for Eloise, and Peggy will need someone with her.'

'What about Tom?'

'I'm sure that her grandmother will make him welcome. I'll let you know.'

He made his usual abrupt departure.

'Most unsatisfactory,' said Francesca to the empty room. She told Lucy, of course, who found it a marvellous idea. 'They have such fun, the boarders—and almost all of my friends are boarders. Do you suppose Mrs Vincent will pay for me?'

'Professor Pitt-Colwyn seemed to think she would. He's going to let me know…'

'Well, of course,' said Lucy airily. 'If they're

in love they'll do anything to please each other. I bet you anything that he'll be back in a few days with everything arranged.'

She was right. Several days later he arrived at teatime, just as they were sitting on the floor in front of the fire, toasting crumpets.

Peggy, no longer spotty but decidedly pasty-faced, rushed to meet him.

'Where have you been? I missed you. Francesca and Lucy missed you too.'

He picked her up and kissed her. 'Well, now I'm here, may I have a cup of tea and one of those crumpets? There's a parcel in the hall for you, too.' He put her down. 'Run and get it; it's from your mother.'

'Will you have a cup of tea?' asked Francesca in a hostess voice and, at his mocking smile and nod, went on, 'Peggy seems to be quite well again, no temperature for three days, but she's so pale…'

She came into the room then with the parcel and began to unwrap it without much enthusiasm. A doll—a magnificent creature, elaborately dressed.

'How very beautiful,' said Francesca. 'You must give her a name. What a lovely present from Mummy.'

'She's like all my other dolls and I don't like any of them. I like my teddy and Tom.' Peggy put the doll carefully on a chair and climbed on to the professor's lap. 'I had a crumpet,' she told him, 'but I can have some of yours, can't I?'

'Provided you don't drip butter all over me and Francesca allows it.'

Francesca passed a large paper serviette over without a word, and poured the fresh tea Lucy had made. That young lady settled herself on the rug before the fire once again and sank her teeth into a crumpet.

'Do tell,' she said. 'Is—?' She caught the professor's eye. 'Oh, yes, of course,' and went on airily, 'Did you have a nice time wherever you went?'

The professor, who had spent exactly twenty-four hours in Birmingham—a city he disliked—only four of which had been in Eloise's company, replied blandly that indeed he had had a most interesting time, as he had a flying visit to Edinburgh and, since heart transplants had often to be dealt with at the most awkward of hours, an all-night session there and, upon his return, another operation in the early hours of the morning at Regent's. Francesca, unaware of this, of course, allowed her imagination to run riot.

She said waspishly, 'I expect a man in your position can take a holiday more or less when he likes. Have another crumpet?'

He took one and allowed Peggy to bite from it before demolishing it.

'There are no more crumpets, I'm afraid,' said Francesca coldly, 'but there is plenty of bread. I can make toast…'

He was sitting back with his eyes closed. 'Delicious—well buttered and spread with Marmite. You know the way to a man's heart, Francesca.'

He opened one eye and smiled at her, but she pretended not to see that and went away to fetch some bread and a pot of Marmite. She put the kettle on again too, foreseeing yet another pot of tea.

The other three were talking about Christmas and laughing a great deal when she got back, and it wasn't until he had at last eaten everything he had been offered that he exchanged a glance with Lucy, who got up at once. 'Peggy! Help me take everything into the kitchen, will you, and we'll wash up? You can have an apron and do the washing; I'll dry.'

Peggy scrambled off the professor's knee. 'You'll not go away?'

'No. What is more, if I'm allowed to, I'll stay until you're in your bed.'

Left alone with him, Francesca cast around in her head for a suitable topic of conversation and came up with, 'Did Mrs Vincent give you any messages for me?'

'None. She thinks it a splendid idea that Peggy should go to her grandmother's for a week or so and that you will go with her. She is quite willing to pay for Lucy to stay at school during that time since she is inconveniencing you. She has asked me to make the arrangements and deal with the travelling and payment of bills and so forth. Oh, and she wishes Mrs Wells to come each day as usual while you're away.'

'Tom Kitten…?'

'He can surely go with you; I can't imagine that Peggy will go without him.'

'No. I'm sure she wouldn't. You reassured Mrs Vincent about Peggy not being well? She's not worried?'

The professor had a brief memory of Eloise's pretty face turning petulant at the threat of her new, exciting life being disrupted. 'No,' he said quietly. 'She is content to leave Peggy in your charge.'

'When are we to go?'

'Sunday morning. That gives you three days in which to pack and leave everything as you would wish it here. I'll telephone Mrs Vincent and talk to her about it; I know that she will be delighted.'

'It won't be too much work for her?'

'She and Mr Vincent have plenty of help. Besides, they love Peggy.'

'Am I to ask Lucy's headmistress if she can board for a week or two?'

'I'll attend to that as well.'

Lucy and Peggy came back then. 'I've washed up,' piped Peggy importantly, 'and now I'm going to have a bath and go to bed. I'll be so very very quick and if you like you can see where my spots were.'

'I look forward to that,' he assured her gravely. 'In ten minutes' time.'

He went as soon as Peggy, bathed and in her nightgown, had solemnly shown him the faint scars from her spots and then bidden him a sleepy goodnight.

His goodbyes were brief, with the remark that he would telephone some time on Saturday to make final arrangements for Sunday.

Lucy was over the moon; she was popular at school and had many friends and, although she had never said so, Francesca was aware that she would like to have been a boarder, and, as for Peggy, when she was told there was no containing her excitement. Something of their pleasure rubbed off on to Francesca and she found herself looking forward to the visit. The future seemed uncertain: there was still no word from Mrs Vincent, although Peggy had had a postcard from Carlisle. There had been no message on it, merely a scrawled, 'Hope you are being a good girl, love Mummy.'

Francesca's efforts to get Peggy to make a crayon drawing for her mother or buy a postcard to send to her came to nought. She wrote to Mrs Vincent's solicitor, enclosing a letter to her and asking him to forward it. She gave a faithful account of Peggy's progress and enclosed an accurate rendering of the money she had spent from the housekeeping allowance, assured her that the little girl was quite well again and asked her to let her know if there was anything special she wished done. The solicitor replied immediately; he understood from Mrs Vincent that it was most unlikely that she would be returning home for some time and Miss Haley was to do whatever she thought was best for Peggy. It wasn't very satisfactory, but Francesca realised that she would have to make the best of it. At least she could call upon the professor again if anything went wrong, and, now that they were going to stay with Peggy's grandparents for a while, they would surely accept responsibility for the child.

The professor telephoned quite early on Saturday morning; he would take Lucy to her school and at the same time have a word with the headmistress. 'Just to make sure that everything is in order,' he explained in what Francesca described to herself as his soothing voice.

'Should I go with you?' she wanted to know.

'No need. I dare say you've already had a few words with her.'

Francesca, feeling guilty, said that yes, she had. 'Just about her clothes and so on,' she said placatingly, and was answered by a mocking grunt.

He arrived on the doorstep in the afternoon with Brontes sitting on the back seat, greeted her with casual civility, assured Peggy that he would take her to her granny's in the morning, waited while Lucy bade Francesca goodbye at some length and then drove her away, refusing politely to return for tea. 'I'm expecting a call from Eloise,' he explained, watching Francesca's face.

Lucy telephoned in the evening; she sounded happy and any doubts that Francesca might have had about her sister's feeling homesick were swept away. She promised to phone herself when they arrived at Peggy's grandparents' house and went away to finish packing.

The professor arrived in time for coffee which Mrs Wells, who had popped round to take the keys and lock up, had ready. He was in an affable mood, answering Peggy's questions with patience while Brontes brooded in a kindly fashion over Tom. Francesca drank her coffee and had nothing to say, conscious that just having the professor there was all she wanted; he annoyed her excessively at times and she didn't think that he liked her overmuch but, all the same, when he was around she felt that there was no need for her to worry about anything. The future was vague—once Mrs Vincent came home she would be out of work again—but then in the meantime she was saving almost every penny of her wages and she liked her job. Moreover, she had become very fond of Peggy.

Rather to her surprise, she was told to sit in the front of the car. 'Brontes will take care of Peggy,' said the professor. 'Tom can sit in the middle in his basket.'

She stayed prudently silent until they joined the M4 where he put a large, well-shod foot down and allowed the car to slide past everything else in the fast lane. 'Just where are we going?' she asked a shade tartly.

'Oh, dear, did I not tell you? But you do know Wiltshire?' When she nodded he added, 'Just on the other side of the Berkshire border. Marlborough is the nearest town. The village is called Nether Tawscombe. They live in the Old Rectory, a charming old place.'

'You've been there before?'

He laughed shortly. 'I spent a number of school holidays there with Jeff and later, when we were at Cambridge and medical school, we spent a good deal of time there.'

'Then he got married,' prompted Francesca.

'Yes. Eloise was never happy there; she dislikes the country.'

Something in his voice stopped her from saying anything more; she turned round to see how the occupants of the back seat were getting on. Peggy had an arm round Brontes's great neck, she had stuck the fingers of her other hand through the mesh in front of Tom's basket and wore an expression of happiness which turned her plain little face into near prettiness. Francesca, who had had secret doubts about the visit, knew that she had been mistaken.

They arrived at Nether Tawscombe in time for lunch. The one village street was empty under the thin, wintry sunshine, but the houses which lined it looked charming. They got larger as the street went uphill until it reached the church, surrounded by a churchyard and ringed around by fair-sized houses. The Old Rectory was close by; an open gate led to a low, rambling house with diamond-paned windows and a solid front door.

As the professor stopped before it, it was

opened and an elderly man came to meet them. She stood a little on one side until Peggy's excited greetings were over and the two men had shaken hands. She was led indoors while the professor saw to their baggage. The hall was stone-flagged, long and narrow, with a door opening on to the garden at the back of the house at its end. Brontes had made straight for it and had been joined by a black Labrador, who had rushed out of an open doorway as a grey-haired lady, cosily plump, had come into the hall.

Peggy screamed with delight and flung herself at her grandmother, and Mr Vincent said to Francesca, 'Always had a soft spot for each other—haven't had her to stay for a long time. This is delightful, Miss—er…?'

'Would you call me Francesca, please? Peggy does.'

Mrs Vincent came to take her hand then, with a warmth which caused sudden tears to prick her eyelids, for the last few years she had been without that kindly warmth…

That the professor was an old friend and welcome guest was evident: he hugged Mrs

Vincent, asked which rooms the bags were to go to, and went up the wide staircase with the air of a man who knew his way about blindfold.

Mrs Vincent saw Francesca's eyes follow him and said comfortably, 'We've known Renier for many years. He and our son were friends; he spent many a school holiday here and Jeff went over to Holland. He's a good man, but I suspect you've discovered that for yourself, Miss…may I call you Francesca?'

'Oh, yes, please. What would you like me to do? Take Peggy upstairs and tidy her for lunch? She's so happy and excited.'

'Yes, dear. You do exactly what you've been doing. We know so little about her day-to-day life now that her father is dead—he brought her here very often, you see.'

No mention of Eloise, reflected Francesca. It wasn't her business, of course. She bore Peggy away upstairs to a couple of low-ceilinged rooms with a communicating door and windows overlooking the wintry garden beyond. After London, even the elegant part of London, it was sheer bliss.

The professor stayed to lunch and she was mystified to hear him say that no, he wasn't going back to London.

'Having a quiet weekend at Pomfritt Cleeve? Splendid,' observed Mr Vincent, and most annoyingly said no more about it.

Renier took his leave soon after lunch, saying goodbye to Francesca last of all, patting her shoulder in an avuncular fashion and remarking casually that he would probably see her at some time. She stood in the hall with everyone else, wishing with all her heart that she were going with him. For that was where she wanted to be, she realised with breathtaking surprise, with him all the time, forever and ever, and, now she came to think about it, she had been in love with him for quite some time, only she had never allowed herself to think about it. Now he was going; not that that would make any difference—he had always treated her at best with friendliness, more often than not with an uninterested politeness.

She looked away so that she didn't see him go through the door.

However sad the state of her heart, she had little time to brood over it. Peggy was a different child, behaving like any normal six-year-old would behave, playing endless games with the Labrador and Tom, racing around the large garden with Francesca in laughing pursuit, going for rides on the elderly donkey who lived in the paddock behind the house, going to the shops in Marlborough with her grandmother and Francesca. She had quickly acquired a splendid appetite and slept the moment her small head touched the pillow. A good thing too, thought Francesca, for by bedtime she was tired herself. She loved her days in the quiet village and Mr and Mrs Vincent treated her like a daughter. Sometimes she felt guilty that she should be living so comfortably while Lucy was in London, although she thought that her sister, from all accounts, was as happy as she was herself. They missed each other, but Francesca had the sense to see that it was good for Lucy to learn independence. She tried not to think of the professor too often and she felt that she was succeeding, until after a week or so Lucy wrote her usual letter and mentioned that he had been to see her at the school and had taken her out to tea. 'To the Ritz, no less!' scrawled Lucy, with a lot of exclamation marks.

The professor, having returned Lucy to her school, went to his home and sat down in his great chair by the fire with Brontes pressed against his knee and mother cat and the kittens asleep in their basket to keep him company. Tea with Lucy had been rewarding and he had made no bones about asking questions, although he had put them in such a way that she hadn't been aware of how much she was telling him. Indeed, she had confided in him that her headmistress had offered her a place in a group of girls from her class going to Switzerland for a skiing holiday. 'But of course I can't go,' she had told him. 'It's a lot of money and Fran couldn't possibly afford it—I mean, we both have to have new winter coats, and if Mrs Vincent comes back we'll have to move again, won't we?'

He had agreed with her gravely, at the same time prising out as much information about the trip as he could. He stroked Brontes's great head. 'I shall have to pay another visit to Eloise,' he told the dog. 'Now how can I fit that in next week?'

Presently he picked up the telephone on the table beside him and dialled a number.

A week, ten days went by. Peggy was so happy that Francesca began to worry about their return; she saw that the child loved her grandparents and they in turn loved her. They didn't spoil her, but she was treated with a real affection which Francesca felt she had never had from her mother. One morning when Peggy had gone off with her grandfather, leaving Francesca to catch up on the washing and ironing of the child's wardrobe, Mrs Vincent came to sit with her in the little room behind the kitchen where the ironing was done. 'You must be wondering why we don't mention Peggy's mother. Oh, I know we talk about her because Peggy must not forget her mother, but you see Eloise never wanted her and when she was born she turned against her—you see she takes after my son, and Eloise was so pretty. She said that her friends would laugh at such an ugly child. It upset Jeff, but she was fortunate—he was a loyal husband; he took Peggy around with him as much as possible and they adored each other. It was a pity that Peggy overheard her mother telling someone one day that she wished the child had not been born. She never told her father, bless the child, but she did tell Mrs Wells, who told me. There is nothing I would like better than to have Peggy to live with us always.'

'Have you suggested it to Eloise?'

'No; you see she will probably marry again and he might like to have Peggy for a daughter.'

Francesca thought Mrs Vincent was talking about the professor. She said woodenly, 'Yes, I dare say that would be very likely.'

It seemed as though it might be true, for the very next day he arrived just as they were sitting down to lunch.

Francesca, going out to the kitchen to ask Bertha, the housekeeper, if she could grill another few chops for their unexpected guest, was glad of her errand: it gave her time to assume the politely cool manner she could hide behind. It was difficult to maintain it, though, for when she got back to the dining-room it was to hear him telling the Vincents that he was on his way to see Eloise. 'I shall be glad of a word with you, sir,' he told Mr Vincent, 'as my visit concerns Peggy, and I think you should know why I am going.'

Francesca ate her chop—sawdust and ashes in her mouth. Afterwards she couldn't remember eating it; nor could she remember what part she took in the conversation during the meal. It must have been normal, for no one looked at her in surprise. She couldn't wait for the professor to be gone, and as though he knew that he sat over coffee, teasing Peggy and having a perfectly unnecessary conversation with Mrs Vincent about the uses of the old-fashioned remedies she used for minor ailments.

He got up at length and went away with Mr

Vincent to the study, to emerge half an hour later and, amid a great chorus of goodbyes, take his leave.

This time Francesca watched him go; when next she saw him he would most likely be engaged to Eloise—even married. She was vague about special licences but, the professor being the man he was, she had no doubt that if he wished to procure one at a moment's notice he would find a way to do so.

It was three days later when Mr Vincent remarked to his wife, 'Renier phoned. He has got his way. He's back in London, but too busy to come down and see us for a few days.'

Mrs Vincent beamed. 'Tell me later—how delightful; he must be very happy.' Francesca, making a Plasticine cat for Peggy, did her best to feel happy, because he was happy, and one should be glad to know that someone one loved was happy, shouldn't one? She found it hard work.

He came at the end of the week, walking in unannounced during a wet afternoon. He looked tired; he worked too hard, thought

Francesca lovingly, scanning the weary lines on his handsome face. He also looked smug—something she found hard to understand.

CHAPTER FIVE

RENIER HAD HAD LUNCH, he assured Mrs Vincent, before going with Mr Vincent to the study again. When they came back into the sitting-room the older man said, 'Well, my dear, it's all settled. Which of us shall tell Peggy?'

'What?' asked Peggy, all ears. 'Is—is it something nice? Like I can stay here forever?'

'You clever girl to guess,' said Mrs Vincent, and gave her a hug. 'That's exactly what you are going to do—live here with Grandpa and me and go to school every day.'

Peggy flung herself at her grandfather. 'Really, truly? I may stay here with you? I won't have to go back to Mummy? She doesn't want me, you know.'

'Well, darling, your mummy is a very busy

person and being on stage is very hard work. You can go and see her whenever you want to,' said Mrs Vincent.

'Shan't want to. Where will Francesca go?'

Francesca went on fixing a tail to another cat and didn't look up. 'If there is no objection, I think it might be a good idea if I took her somewhere quiet and explained everything to her,' said the professor.

He added gently, 'Get your coat, Francesca, and come with me.'

'Now that is a good idea,' said Mrs Vincent. 'Run along, dear; Renier will explain everything to you so much better than we can.'

There was no point in refusing; she fetched her old Burberry and went out to the car with him, to be greeted with pleasure by Brontes, who was roaming the garden. The professor opened the door and stuffed her gently into her seat, got in beside her and, with Brontes's great head wedged between their shoulders, drove off.

'Where am I going?' asked Francesca coldly.

'Pomfritt Cleeve. I have a cottage there. We can talk quietly.'

'What about? Surely you could have told me at Mrs Vincent's house?'

'No, this concerns you as well as Peggy.'

He had turned off the main road into a narrow, high-hedged lane going downhill, and presently she saw a cluster of lights through the gathering dusk. A minute or so later they had reached the village—one street with a church halfway along, a shop or two, and small, old cottages, well maintained—before he turned into another narrow lane, and after a hundred yards or so drove through a propped-open gate and stopped before a thatched cottage of some size. There were lights in the windows and the door was thrown open as she got out of the car, hesitating for a moment, giving Brontes time to rush through the door with a delighted bark, almost knocking down the stout little lady standing there. She said, 'Good doggie,' in a soft, West Country voice and then added, 'Come on in out of the cold, sir, and the young lady. There's a good fire in the sitting-room and tea in ten minutes.'

The professor flung an arm around her cosy person and kissed her soundly. 'Blossom, how very nice to see you again—and something smells delicious.'

He caught Francesca gently by the arm. 'Francesca, this is Blossom, who lives here and looks after the cottage for me. Blossom, this is Miss Haley. Take her away so that she can tidy herself if she wants to, and we'll have tea in ten minutes, just as you say.'

The cottage, decided Francesca, wasn't a cottage really. It might look like one, but it was far too big to warrant such a name, although there was nothing grand about it. The sitting-room to which she was presently shown was low-ceilinged with comfortable chairs and tables dotted around on the polished floor. There was a low table before the fire and sofas on either side of it. She sat opposite her host, pouring tea into delicate china cups and eating scones warm from the oven and, having been well brought up, made light conversation.

However, not for long. 'Let us dispense with the small talk,' said the professor, 'and get down to facts. Eloise is quite happy to allow Peggy to live with her grandparents. She will of course be free to see the child whenever she wishes, but she will remarry very shortly and intends to stay on the stage, so it isn't likely that she will visit Peggy more than once in a while. Mrs Vincent will employ her old nanny's daughter to look after Peggy, so you may expect to leave as soon as she arrives.' Francesca gave a gasp, but he went on, 'Don't interrupt, I have not yet finished. Lucy has been told that she may join a school party going to Switzerland to ski—I have seen her headmistress and she will join the party.'

'Now look here,' said Francesca, and was hushed once more.

'I haven't said anything to you, for I knew that you would refuse to do anything about it. The child deserves a holiday and, as for the costs, you can repay me when you are able.'

'But I haven't got a job,' said Francesca wildly. 'I never heard such arrogance—going behind my back and making plans and arranging things—'

'Ah, yes, as to arrangements for yourself, Eloise is quite agreeable to your remaining at the cottage for a few days so that you can pack your things.'

She goggled at him, bereft of words. That she loved him dearly went without saying, but at the moment she wished for something solid to throw at him. 'You have been busy, haven't you?' she said nastily.

'Yes, indeed I have. I shall drive Lucy over to Zeebrugge to meet the school party there; you would like to come with us, no doubt.'

'How can I? I'll have to look for a job—'

'Well, as to that, I have a proposal to make.' He was sitting back, watching her, smiling faintly.

'Well, I don't want to hear it,' she declared roundly. 'I shan't listen to anything more you may say—'

'Perhaps this isn't the right time, after all. You are cross, are you not? But there is really nothing you can do about it, is there? You will break young Lucy's heart if you refuse to let her go to Switzerland—'

'She had no skiing clothes.'

'Now she has all she needs—a Christmas present.'

She all but ground her teeth. 'And I suppose you're going to get married?'

'That is my intention.'

Rage and despair almost choked her, and she allowed rage to take over.

'I hope you will be very happy.' Her voice was icy and not quite steady.

'I am certain of that.'

'I'd like to go back.' He agreed at once, which was a good thing—otherwise she might have burst into tears. Where was she to go? And there was Lucy to think of when she got back from Switzerland. Would she have time to get a job by then? And would her small hoard of money be sufficient to keep them until she had found work again? There were so many questions to be answered. Perhaps she should have listened to this proposal he had mentioned—it could have been another job—but pride wouldn't allow her to utter another word. She bade Blossom goodbye, complimented her on her scones and got into the car; it smelled comfortingly of leather and, very faintly, of Brontes.

Strangely enough, the great bulk of the professor beside her was comforting too, although she could think of no good reason why it should be.

Back at the Vincent's house after a silent drive, he bade them goodbye, bent his great height to Peggy's hug, observed cheerfully to Francesca that he would be in touch, and left.

She had no idea what he had said to the Vincents, but from what they said she gathered that they understood her to have a settled future, and there seemed no point in enlightening them. Peggy, chattering excitedly as Francesca put her to bed, seemed to think that she would see her as often as she wanted, and Francesca said nothing to disillusion her. The future was her own problem.

She left the Vincents two days later, and was driven back to the mews cottage by Mr Vincent. She hated leaving the quiet village. Moreover, she had grown very fond of Peggy who, even while bidding her a tearful goodbye, was full of plans to see her again, which were seconded by her grandmother. She had responded suitably and kept up a cheerful conversation with her companion as they drove but, once he had left her at the empty house, with the observation that they would be seeing each other shortly, she sat down in the kitchen and had a good cry. She felt better after that, made a cup of tea, and unpacked before starting on the task of re-packing Lucy's cases as well as her own. There had been a brief letter for her before she left the Vincents', telling her that they would be crossing over to Zeebrugge in two days' time, and would she be ready to leave by nine o'clock in the morning and not a minute later?

Mrs Wells had kept the place spotless, and there was a note on the kitchen table saying that she would come in the morning; there was a little ironing and nothing else to do but pack. She was halfway through that when Lucy phoned.

'You're back. Isn't it exciting? I can't believe

it's true. I'm coming home tomorrow after-
noon. The bus leaves here in the evening, but
Renier says he'll take us to Zeebrugge early
the next day and I can join the others there.
Isn't he a darling?' She didn't wait for
Francesca's answer, which was just as well.
'Oh, Fran, I do love being a boarder. I know I
can't be, but you have no idea what fun it is.
I've been asked to lots of parties at Christmas,
too.'

Francesca let her talk. There was time
enough to worry over the problem of
Christmas; she still had almost three weeks to
find a job and somewhere for them to live,
too.

'You're very quiet,' said Lucy suddenly.

'I've had a busy day; I'm packing for us both
now—I'll do the rest tomorrow. I've got to
talk to Mrs Wells, too.'

'I'll help you. You are looking forward to the
trip, aren't you?'

'Tremendously,' said Francesca with her
fingers crossed. 'See you tomorrow, Lucy.'

By the time Lucy arrived, she had done everything that was necessary. Mrs Wells had been more than helpful, arranging to come early in the morning to take the keys and lock up. The solicitor had been dealt with, she had been to the bank and taken out as much money as she dared, found their passports—unused since they had been on holiday in France with their parents—and, finally, written a letter to Mrs Vincent which she had enclosed in a letter to the solicitor. There was nothing more to do but have a good gossip and go to bed.

The Bentley purred to a halt outside the cottage at precisely nine o'clock, then the professor got out, wished them an affable good-morning, put Francesca's overnight bag and Lucy's case in the boot, enquired as to what had been done with the rest of their luggage—safely with Mrs Wells—and urged them to get in. 'You go in front, Lucy,' said Francesca and nipped into the back seat, not seeing his smile, and resolutely looked out of the window all the way to Dover, trying not to listen to the cheerful talk between the other two.

Five hours later they were in Zeebrugge,

driving to the hotel where the rest of the party had spent the night, and it was only then that she realised that she had no idea what was to happen next. There wasn't any time to think about it; the bus was ready to leave. It was only after a hasty goodbye to Lucy, when she was watching the party drive away, that the full awkwardness of the situation dawned upon her. 'Whatever am I going to do?' She had turned on the professor, her voice shrill with sudden fright. 'When is there a boat back?'

He took her arm. 'We are going to my home in Holland for the night. My mother will be delighted to meet you.'

'I must get back—I have to find a job.'

He took no notice, merely urged her gently into the car, got in beside her and drove off.

'This is ridiculous...I've been a fool—I thought we would be going straight back. I'm to spend the night at Mrs Wells's house.'

'We will telephone her.' His voice was soothing as well as matter-of-fact. 'We shall soon be home.'

They were already through Brugge and on

the motorway, bypassing Antwerp, crossing into Holland, and racing up the Dutch motorways to Tilburg, Nijmegen and on past Arnhem. The wintry afternoon was turning to an early dusk and, save for a brief halt for coffee and sandwiches, they hadn't stopped. Francesca, trying to make sense of the situation, sat silent, her mind addled with tiredness and worry and a deep-seated misery, because once they were back in England there would be no reason to see the professor ever again. The thought cast her in such deep gloom that she barely noticed the country had changed; the road ran through trees and thick shrubbery with a light glimpsed here and there. The professor turned off the road through a gateway, slowed along a narrow, sanded drive and stopped before the house at its end. He leaned over, undid her safety belt, got out and helped her out too, and she stood for a moment, looking at the dark bulk of the house. It was square and solid, its big windows lighted, frost sparkling on the iron balcony above the porch.

She said in a forlorn voice, 'I should never

have come with you. I should never have let you take over my life, and Lucy's, too. I'm very grateful for your help; you have been kind and I expect it suited you and Eloise. I can't think why you've brought me here.'

'You wouldn't listen to my proposal at Pomfritt Cleeve,' the professor had come very close, 'I can see that I shall have to try again.' He put his arms around her and held her very close. 'You are a stubborn, proud girl with a beautiful head full of muddled thoughts, and I love you to distraction. I fell in love with you the first time I saw you, and what is all this nonsense about Eloise? I don't even like the woman, but something had to be done about Peggy. Now you will listen, my darling, while I make you a proposal. Will you marry me?'

What with his great arms around her and her heart thumping against her ribs, Francesca hadn't much breath—only just enough to say, 'Yes, oh, yes, Renier,' before he bent to kiss her.